PRAISE FOR
SITTING ON A FILE CABINET, NAKED, WITH A GUN

Is clairvoyance a job prerequisite for executive assistants? With humor, variety, and practical tips, *Sitting on a File Cabinet, Naked, With a Gun* is an easy read that illustrates the impact of great CEO/Executive Assistant teamwork.

> — *Aart de Geus, chairman of the Board and Chief Executive Officer, Synopsys, Inc.*

The stories in this book paint an accurate picture of the trials and tribulations of an executive assistant's professional life. These true-life scenarios and the lessons learned will benefit any assistant aspiring to greatness while dealing with the day-to-day realities. Joanne Linden and Linda McFarland are savvy executive assistants who know what it takes to be successful in this fascinating career.

> — *Joan Burge, founder and CEO, Office Dynamics, Ltd., and author*

Insight, ethics, sense of humor, trust—an executive's assistant can make or break him. A great assistant makes *everyone* feel special (but more importantly, not necessarily the boss, who needs an honest partner, not a cheerleader). When you find one who is world class, the teamwork can be truly amazing. Told using real-world stories, this book will help all professionals wanting to excel as an executive assistant.

> — *Jeff Rodek, senior lecturer, The Ohio State University Fisher College of Business and former Chairman & CEO, Hyperion*

In *Sitting on a File Cabinet, Naked, With a Gun*, these authors have taken the ultimate risk in talking about their complex and amazing profession. They have courageously taught, mentored, trained, and supported professional assistants for years. Now at last, they present the stories, hints, and tools it takes to serve a powerful and innovative

leader of his field. Garnered from each ounce of blood, sweat, and tears they gave, the results are digestible to those from all sides of the desk. Linda and Joanne are ready to give away the secrets that made them so successful in their corporate endeavors. The lessons hurt, tickle, infuse, and comfort every single person who tries to make other executive professionals' lives work!

— Jean Hollands, MS, founder of Growth & Leadership Center,
author of Same Game/Different Rules

This is a must-read for administrative assistants and all CEOs to learn tips for developing and enhancing one of the key partnerships in their careers. Having worked as a conflict mediator and executive coach for many years, I find the authors' wisdom and insights invaluable. The stories are funny, engaging, and instructive. You won't be able to put it down.

— Marilyn Manning, Ph.D., CEO, The Consulting Team, LLC

Joanne and Linda have tapped into what assistants really deal with every day! These true stories will motivate you, surprise you, and make you laugh. This book sheds new light on the complex and vital role of the assistant in today's corporate world. I couldn't get enough of the stories of demanding bosses, unimaginable duties, exciting successes, and just plain entertaining examples from some of the best in the business. It's a creative approach and a must-read for every assistant and his or her boss!

— Lisa Olsen, professional development specialist and
motivational speaker

Sitting on a File Cabinet, Naked, With a Gun

True Stories of Silicon Valley CEO Assistants

Linda McFarland & Joanne Linden
with Sharon Turnoy

authorHOUSE®

AuthorHouse™
1663 Liberty Drive
Bloomington, IN 47403
www.authorhouse.com
Phone: 1-800-839-8640

First published by AuthorHouse 10/27/2009

ISBN: 978-1-4490-3160-2 (e)
ISBN: 978-1-4490-3159-6 (sc)
ISBN: 978-1-4490-3158-9 (hc)

Library of Congress Control Number: 2009909992

Printed in the United States of America
Bloomington, Indiana

This book is printed on acid-free paper.

Cover design by Richard K. McDaniel Graphic Design.

TABLE OF CONTENTS

DEDICATION

I dedicate this book to my parents – to my father, Edward Harvanec (1915-1995), for his example that even an introvert can be very successful in a people-oriented business, and to my mother, Helen Harvanec, for taking me to her workplace and inspiring me to follow in her footsteps.

I dedicate this book as well to my husband, Allan, for believing in me and encouraging me to reach ever higher, and to my children, Ashley and Robert, who think I'm crazy for taking on yet one more thing, but are proud of me for doing so.

– Joanne Linden

I dedicate this book to my mom and dad, Joanne and Leon Collett, to my siblings, Elaine, Daniel, Teresa, Cathleen, Samuel, and Juliann, to my husband, Tim, and to my children, Melissa, Timmy, Bryan, and Shawn.

Growing up in a family with seven children, my childhood was filled with many extraordinary and memorable events. I remember my mother once saying that, with all our adventures, she could write a book! Unfortunately, cancer claimed her at the young age of 56, and her book was never to be. Aside from a few entries in her journal, she never did write down those incredible stories. Although this book isn't about my family's stories, her idea inspired me to turn some awkward and humorous work situations into stories of adventure and intrigue.

My ever-so-patient family has spent many dinner hours hearing my tales of corporate life. They always listened with rapt attention, or at least they pretended to. Either way, they inspired me to finally put pen to paper and share with the world the humor, challenges, and sometimes tears that corporate America has thrown my way. For their support, I am eternally grateful to them.

– Linda McFarland

FOREWORD

The life of an executive assistant is sometimes perceived as "just something you do until something better comes along." Nothing could be further from the truth. Being an executive assistant is a career filled with opportunity, entertainment, and perpetual movement. Any individual who thinks that anyone can do this job does not understand the role. To be the executive assistant working side by side with an influential CEO offers challenges that are sometimes beyond comprehension unless you have been there yourself.

Joanne Linden and Linda McFarland's book is packed with wonderful, true stories of what really happens behind the closed doors of the executive suite. You will be privy to situations that you never imagined could happen, but they do. They will make you laugh, gasp for breath, or say, "I've felt that way, too."

For those of you who are already working with a C-level executive, you will find gems of wisdom laced throughout the book. For those of you who aspire to move into the executive suite, this can be a roadmap guiding you to the skills and attitudes required to be successful when you arrive. As you read the stories, be sure to look for the lessons learned, as they do not appear only in the *Points of Wisdom*™ *(POW!*™*)* at the end of each chapter, but throughout the entire book.

I have been privileged to know Joanne and Linda since 2006. As someone who worked in the administrative profession for 20 years and has been training administrative assistants since 1990, I can attest to their level of expertise. They know what it takes to be a successful CEO's partner.

They are passionate about their profession, and through this book, they will help others in their field excel. Be prepared to learn and laugh as you explore what goes on behind the scenes in the executive suite!

Joan Burge, founder and CEO
Office Dynamics

ACKNOWLEDGMENTS

This book was a long time in coming, four-and-a-half years to be precise (but who's counting?). We went into this endeavor without a clue as to how to write or publish a book. We quickly found that we needed much advice, mentoring, and encouragement. Some of the people who helped in those areas are Kimberly Wiefling, Dr. Marilyn Manning, Kathi Fox, Kathy Schmidt, Joan Burge, Jean Hollands, Randy Peyser, and Lisa Olsen.

We interviewed many CEO assistants to gather their stories and anecdotes. We weren't able to fit every story in our book, but we're grateful for all their contributions nonetheless. They are Bonnie Savage, Sherry Parsons, Carol Ochoa, Dee Hartman, Marie Simmons, Cindy Silva, Luda Selasco, Pam Shore, Marilyn Pfarr, Helena Bradley, Sande Guenther, Georgia Brint, Dorothy Connell, Michele Valentine, Ann Christensen, and Debbie Gross.

A special thanks to the CEOs who approved the use of their names in our stories, as well as those who appear in our pages unidentified. Without them, this book would not have been possible. It is because of them that we have become the executive assistants that we are today.

Sharon Turnoy joined us as our editor about a year into our journey and gave our stories the "zing" that had been missing. And as a former CEO assistant herself, she was able to mind-read what we really meant to say.

Thank you to our friends who kept inquiring about how the book was going and for not letting us see your eyes glaze over when we went into too much detail. (But you asked.)

We saved the most important people for last—our families. Thank you for your patience while we spent nights and weekends meeting in each other's homes. A special thanks to our husbands, Tim McFarland and Allan Linden, for feeding us countless meals during those meetings. Thank you for encouraging us not to give up when we felt overwhelmed. Thank you for reading all those stories time and time again, even if we changed only a word here and there. Thank you for laughing in the right places. Thank you for being our biggest fans.

INTRODUCTION

"As you become more clear about who you really are, you'll be better able to decide what is best for you – the first time around."
– Oprah Winfrey

Sitting on a File Cabinet, Naked, With a Gun is a book about a small group of women who wield an enormous amount of power—the executive assistants to the CEOs of Silicon Valley, California. If you've ever wondered what goes on behind the closed doors of the executive suite in the high-tech capital of the world, we will tell you. Some of the most powerful men and women are represented in these stories, as executive assistants spill the beans about their CEOs.

This is a book for all business managers, not just administrative professionals. It will ring as true for the "newbie admin" as the seasoned assistant who's been around more years than she would care to admit. Managers at all levels will come away with a better understanding of the intricacies of the CEO's office and how to interact with it.

Executive assistants are arguably the most influential people on a chief executive's staff. They are historically a "secret weapon" — typically, not even recognized for their ability to influence the CEO. Too often, they are written off as "just a secretary." Beware of making that outdated mistake!

Today's CEO executive assistants are engaged in *all* aspects of the business. They leverage their CEOs' highly valuable time so they can devote their total energies to making the major strategic decisions for their companies. These assistants continually seek out ways to make their jobs more enriching, more efficient, and more empowering. Readers will hear the tale of an assistant who saved a CEO's life, another who kept her CEO from being turned away from the White House, and one who even finessed a major deal for the company.

Sitting on a File Cabinet, Naked, With a Gun is especially useful for anyone who has his or her eye on a spot reporting to a CEO one day. After each slice-of-life anecdote, there are informative "Points of Wisdom," or "POW!," which are a useful guide for anyone who comes in contact with the CEO's office.

Unlike other books addressed to all levels of administrative assistants, the true value in *Sitting on a File Cabinet* is our first-hand understanding of what it takes to be the assistant to the CEO of a billion-dollar corporation. In addition, we have filled the book with a feast of funny, occasionally shocking, sometimes moving, but, we hope, always entertaining stories about the real human beings "at the top." These stories reveal how we and our peers became key influencers of some of the world's top CEOs, and how we manage to keep our cool (or occasionally don't) as we navigate high-pressure situations on an hourly basis.

SITTING ON A FILE CABINET, NAKED, WITH A GUN

Joanne Linden, chief executive assistant at Synopsys, shares a story about a colleague at a prior company, Carol, who worked in the chaotic environment of high finance. At fiscal year-end, Carol was being pulled in all directions. Her stress level was at its peak when a coworker intervened with a story about a former colleague—an executive assistant to a CEO who had an unusual way of handling stress.

"It's not stress that kills us; it is our reaction to it." – Hans Selye

My friend Carol, whom I've known for 17 years, is the epitome of the cool, calm, and collected executive assistant. She's flawlessly groomed, utterly competent, and maintains a patient smile on her face at all times.

What's surprising is that she maintains this demeanor in a crazy environment—finance. You may not think that a bunch of accountants with calculators in their pocket protectors would be a particularly wild group, but when the end of the fiscal year approaches, watch out! Stress levels reach their peak, and there's a constant line of people at Carol's desk, each insisting on bringing something to the CFO's attention immediately.

One day, my coworker "Cheryl" and I found Carol in the break room, slamming cabinet doors and cursing: "Where the *@!# is the chamomile tea? Nothing is ever where it's supposed to be. Am I the only one who puts things back where they belong? This whole place is a mess."

Cheryl and I exchanged glances. This was not the Carol we knew and loved. Cheryl plunged in, "Having a bad day, honey?"

Carol grimaced, "It's fiscal year end. Need I say more? If I have one more investor relations prima donna trying to barge into John's office without going through me, I'm going to murder him—or her. I literally had to throw myself in front of John's door just now to keep Her Royal Highness Miss Princess Know-It-All from busting in. You know who I mean. I told her John gave me strict orders not to disturb him under *any* circumstances. She gave me a tongue-lashing and told me that if the stock takes a dive because I insisted on following 'protocol,' she would make sure everyone knows it was my fault. Now, where the hell is the chamomile tea?"

Cheryl walked past Carol to a cabinet under the sink. "I have a secret stash under here," Cheryl cooed. "Why don't you take a seat, girlfriend, and I'll make this cup for you." Cheryl put her arm maternally around Carol's petite shoulders and guided her to a table. She pulled the chair out for her, sat her down, patted her perfectly coiffed head, then went back to the sink to make three cups of tea. Meanwhile, I sat down next to Carol and tried to get her to take some slow, deep breaths.

Cheryl brought the tea over and took a seat. "Carol, would you like to hear about a coworker I once had? She had kind of an unusual way of handling her stress. It might be just what the doctor ordered for you right now."

Carol took a sip of tea and just nodded, with utter defeat written on her face. It was clear to Carol that nothing would help, but she was willing at least to pretend to listen. I turned to Cheryl with a look of anticipation, ready to hear another one of her infamous stories. (It seemed that Cheryl had an endless supply.)

"I used to work at a small start-up," Cheryl began, "which shall remain nameless to protect the 'guilty.' One of the women there—I'll call her 'Sheila'—was the executive assistant to the CEO, but she had to wear lots of other hats as well. She always seemed on the verge of a nervous breakdown because she worked day and night with no let-up. She didn't know how to say 'no' when it came to her workload, and the stress would *really* get to her. Occasionally, she would blow up at someone, but she always recovered, except for this one time.

"One evening, as everyone was leaving, Sheila was still at her desk, trying to finish a report for a board meeting the next day. Apparently, she didn't have all the information she needed to complete the report, and she was in a total panic. Talk about stress! She was so far gone that when I asked her if there was anything I could do to help, she just mumbled something unintelligible and waved her arms at me to go away. I'm not sure if she even heard me; but either way, I got the message to steer clear.

"The next morning, the CEO was the first to arrive. Well, Sheila had never gone home. As he walked in the front door, she was directly in front of him, sitting on a file cabinet, naked, with a gun."

At this point, Cheryl sat back and took a long sip of her tea. She raised her eyes, looked slowly at Carol, then at me, and put the teacup down. Both of us were frozen in our seats, with our jaws dropped.

After the initial shock, Carol was the first to recover. "I guess I don't have it that bad after all. But if you see me going near a file cabinet, stop me, okay?" At that remark, we all laughed.

From then on, whenever Cheryl, Carol, or I realized we were having an especially stressful day, we would call up one of the other two and simply say, "I'm heading for the file cabinet."

The other would reply, "Do you still have your clothes on?"

If the answer was "yes," we knew all would be well. But the phone call—and especially the visual that came to mind—would make us both laugh, and the stress would dissipate.

Carol and I have stayed in touch over the years, and we still use that tactic to this day. I'm not sure what either of us would do if the answer to the question, "Do you still have your clothes on?" turned out to be "No." Thankfully, that hasn't happened yet.

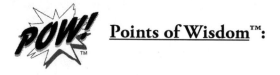 **<u>Points of Wisdom</u>**™:

- Find a humorous tool you can use to break the tension whenever you feel close to going over the edge.
- Be willing to accept support from colleagues to make it through an immediate crisis.

AN IRON FIST IN A VELVET GLOVE

Linda McFarland shares a story about her bumpy rise to her first CEO assistant position.

**"Justice and power must be brought together,
so that whatever is just may be powerful,
and whatever is powerful may be just." – Blaise Pascal**

I began my secretarial career at 17, when I was recruited for my first job at our high school job fair. Somewhere along the way, I managed to go to a university for a year, but the demands of a full-time job, a university education, and a brand-new husband forced me to re-evaluate my choices. Something had to give.

I wasn't about to give up my husband; but between college and work, I enjoyed work more. Besides, work brought money in, while college just took it out. In a parallel universe somewhere, I have an MBA. But in this one, I never did finish my undergraduate degree.

Over the next few years, I worked my way up through the ranks as a secretary and eventually supported high-level division managers and executives at a large company.

After four years, when I left to take a position supporting the CFO at a local hospital, I realized how much I truly enjoyed supporting C-level executives. I learned more about the inside workings of the business in this spot than I had in any of my prior lower-level positions. My ambition to become a CEO's assistant was born right then and there.

Unfortunately, the woman currently in that position had planted barbed wire firmly around her territory. So I eventually left to take a position supporting the branch president at a nationwide office furniture supplier. The CFO at the hospital tried to talk me out of leaving. He said I was the best assistant he'd ever had, and he didn't know how he would replace me. Though I felt a little guilty, since he had done a lot for my development, I was determined to pursue my dream.

As fate would have it, just after I arrived at the furniture supply company, my new boss got caught in the crossfire of a corporate restructure. Within three days of starting my new job, he was demoted. I had no idea if I even had a job, much less one supporting an executive. I called the CFO at the hospital and asked him, "Will you still take me back?" He hadn't filled the position yet and was ecstatic to hear from me.

As ours was a small hospital, the CEO routinely signed off on all the executive assistant hires and terminations. The CFO approached the CEO, fully expecting that my reinstatement would be a no-brainer.

However, life takes an unexpected turn occasionally, and this happened to be one of those times. Neither of us knew that the CEO's assistant was relieved when I left. She probably sensed my career ambition and felt threatened by it, so she "poisoned the well." When she learned that I was hoping to return, she told the CEO that I was returning because I "couldn't cut it" at the new company, and that the hospital shouldn't take back any "losers." Due to this woman's slander, the net result was that, despite the CFO's protestations, my reinstatement was not approved.

Although being dealt such a blow, I ended up in a good position after all. Everything worked out well at my new job with the furniture supply company. The new branch president decided to keep me as his assistant, and we developed a great partnership. My experiences with him strengthened my skills to support a CEO whenever the opportunity arose.

After just two years, the hospital I had formerly worked for went through a reorganization of its own. The CEO who had rejected my reinstatement departed, and without the CEO around to protect her, it was only a matter of time before his former executive assistant was terminated.

The newly appointed CEO at the hospital needed an executive assistant, and he asked the CFO for recommendations. My former boss didn't waste any time in calling me. He brought me up to date on the changes at the hospital and asked if I would be interested in coming back to interview for the CEO assistant position.

Was I interested? Wild horses couldn't keep me away!

During my interview, the new CEO explained that he had been sent by the corporate office to clean up a number of management and budgetary problems, as well as to implement some pilot programs. He had no less than 49 major action items to take care of in 18 months and told me that he needed to find someone with enough initiative and energy not just to keep up with his projects, but to stay one step ahead of him.

In addition, the CEO was very concerned with the political situation that had developed under the previous administration. He asked some very pointed questions to determine whether I would be likely to abuse the inherent power of my position. I answered honestly, point for point, and I must have satisfied him that my motives were pure.

Perhaps to ensure that I wouldn't get too full of myself, he asked, "What do you think about being called an 'executive secretary' instead of a 'CEO assistant'?" Though my heart sank a little, I bravely replied that the title wasn't as important as the opportunity that the position represented.

Within a week, I was hired. I was thrilled when I received the offer. Ten years into my career, I had finally landed the CEO assistant position.

As my new executive had previously informed me, I was given the title of executive secretary. That didn't keep him from treating me like a full-fledged assistant who was expected to make independent decisions and manage an extremely busy office. He came to depend on me more and more with each passing day.

About five months into the job, the CEO called me into his office. "Do you remember during our interview when we talked about your title and my concerns about the potential abuse of power if we called you a 'CEO assistant'?"

I was floored. I had been scrupulously careful to ensure that I hadn't thrown around the weight of the executive's title. I had done my very best to be helpful and friendly to everyone equally, and I certainly had never spread any gossip. I racked my brain to see whether anything I might have said or done in the past five months could possibly have been interpreted as political or toxic.

I'm not sure how much time passed as those five months flashed before my eyes. I suddenly realized the CEO was waiting for my answer. I somehow managed to croak out, "Yes, I remember."

The CEO continued: "You seemed so confident in the interview that I wanted to see if you could prove yourself. I know you've been here only a short time, but you have not only proven yourself; you have actually exceeded my expectations." With that, he informed me that he had already authorized a bonus check, a raise, and a title change to CEO Assistant.

It took a moment for it to register that he had called me in to reward me, not to reprimand me. As the realization sank in, my face broke into a big smile.

Within 18 months, the CEO had accomplished every one of his 49 action items and was getting ready to return to corporate headquarters. I was very flattered when he tried to convince me to come with him, especially since this had been my first CEO assistant position. He told me that I accomplished more in one day than two assistants would at the corporate office. I was tempted by the offer, but did not want to move across the country with four kids and a husband who were firmly settled in Silicon Valley.

He reluctantly accepted my decision to stay, but he left me with an important gift. Over the years, I have reflected on the lesson I learned about not crossing the line while wielding the power one commands as a CEO's assistant.

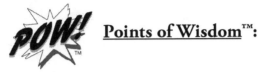 **Points of Wisdom™:**

- Don't let the title of a position get in the way of your dreams and goals; hard work will pay off.
- Respect the power of the position you command.
- Be professional, maintain your integrity, and hold high values.
- Be proactive, use good judgment, and strive to become a partner to the CEO. The respect you earn will put you in a league apart from the traditional administrative role.

WHAT WAS I THINKING!?!

Joanne Linden knew from an early age that she wanted to be an administrative assistant, but it took a twist of fate to land her the role of executive assistant to a CEO.

"You are never given a dream without also being given the power to make it true..." – Richard Bach

I remember as if it were yesterday going to work once with my mother when I was nine years old. It was summer break, and on that day, none of my older brothers and sisters could take care of me. My mom had no choice but to drag me along with her and hope that I wouldn't be too much of a nuisance. (Little did she know that she was decades ahead of the nation's future "Take Your Daughter to Work Day.")

Mom was the only secretary at a small tool-and-die company in Cleveland. While I watched, a constant stream of people came to her desk, from the president to the receptionist, each one asking for her expertise in some matter. Until that day, I had no idea that she ran that company! She certainly had to be the most important person there, because no one seemed capable of doing their jobs without her.

That was the day I knew I wanted to be a secretary, just like my mom. (Or maybe it was because they had free donuts.)

I began my secretarial career directly out of high school. I was fortunate. Each position provided more responsibilities and regular promotions. My career was advancing and I felt fulfilled—that is, until I met my mentor, Dick Clark (no, not the host from *American Bandstand* and *New Year's Rockin' Eve*).

Dick Clark was the vice president of an RF (radio frequency) and microwave components manufacturing company, and I became his assistant. Up until that point, in a career of almost 15 years, I had always taken direction from my boss, waiting for him to tell me what he wanted me to do next.

Dick was different. He wanted me to manage *him*, not the other way around. Dick taught me to think ahead and anticipate his needs. At first, this was very difficult. What did he think I was—a mind reader?

Eventually, after a lot of hits and misses, I got better at this skill and could anticipate his needs to the point where other people thought I actually *could* read Dick's mind. This ability opened up a whole new world for me.

Dick became my first real mentor. He was very discerning about people's potential, and he took the time to explain the business to me—not just the products, but also the politics. None of my bosses before him had recognized that I was bright enough to understand all that information, as well as apply it to help make his job easier. Dick believed that I could go far. In fact, I'm sure he believed in me more than I believed in myself at the time.

Each year during my review, Dick would ask me what I wanted to do in the future. That was a bit of a mixed message. I was flattered that he thought I was capable enough to do whatever I set my sights on, but I also felt a little bit as though being a secretary, in his opinion, somehow wasn't good enough for me.

This wasn't the first time that I had run into the stigma associated with my career. It was hard not to internalize the feeling I got from others that I was "just a secretary." That's probably why most of my bosses hadn't shared that much of their business with me in the past.

12

After all, I was a secretary *and* a blonde. How could I possibly have a brain in my head?

Although it would be years before I started campaigning for a new level of respect for professional administrators, something within me already rebelled at this type of stereotyping. And to have this bias come even subtly from Dick hurt me deeply, because this was the guy who thought I was really talented, so I wanted him especially to respect my career choice. I really liked what I was doing. I was good at it, and I had finally gotten to where I wanted to be. Why would I want to do anything else? But this was all taking place in the late 1980s; and I realize now, with the benefit of hindsight, that there was a lot of consciousness still to be raised.

In my third year working for Dick, I decided to surprise him at review time. I wanted him to stop asking me what I wanted to be when I grew up. When he asked the inevitable question, I thought I would shock Dick so that he would never ask me again. "Actually, I plan to become the assistant to the president of the company," I vowed.

Without missing a beat, Dick replied, "That's great news, because I plan to become the president of the company."

That sure wasn't the answer I had expected! Now I was stuck with my vow.

Soon after our conversation, Dick embarked on a behind-the-scenes campaign to get the board to consider replacing the current president. It wasn't unreasonable to think that Dick might be considered. As a talented turnaround specialist, whenever a business unit or division was not meeting results, Dick was sent in to reverse the trend. He had proven his value many times over.

Just when Dick thought he had won over a majority of the board, word got back to the president. Poor Dick! The political fecal matter hit the fan. Favors were called in and arms were twisted, with the net result that Dick was summarily marched out the door.

I was devastated. My mentor was gone. My husband couldn't understand why I cried every night for a week. But unless you have experienced a boss like Dick, no one can understand. I didn't think I would ever find anyone that I could work with like that again.

Meanwhile back at the components company, I finally pulled myself together and decided that life must go on. I was going to keep up my end of the bargain with Dick and fulfill my vow. I continued on my mission to become an executive assistant to the president of a large corporation.

First, I took a look at my resume to see what I could do to beef it up. I began taking classes at the local junior college—business communications, accounting, and business law—to sharpen my business acumen. I decided to join Professional Secretaries International (now known as the "International Association of Administrative Professionals"), because I wanted to network with other people who considered administrative work a bona fide profession. Through PSI, I studied for and passed the Certified Professional Secretary exam.

One of the benefits of belonging to PSI was that members shared job opportunities at our monthly meetings. At one of these, I heard about a position for an executive assistant to the chairman and CEO of a local telecommunications company. It just so happened that the new vice president of human resources there was an ex-colleague of mine. I figured that knowing the VP in charge of recruiting should come in handy! In these days before email became ubiquitous, I sent my resume via "snail mail" and confidently waited for him to recognize my name and respond.

So much for knowing people in high places! A month went by and nothing happened. Disappointed and discouraged, I increasingly lost confidence in my qualifications for this kind of step up the career ladder. I finally mustered enough courage to pick up the phone and call him. At the least, I wanted to find out what I should do to fix my resume and make myself more marketable for the next time such an opportunity arose.

It turned out that he had not dismissed me out of hand, as I had feared. He had never gotten my resume! In a month's time, my resume hadn't even made it into the candidate pool. Who knows in which recruiter's in-box it had gotten stuck? The VP told me to send it right away, to his attention, and he'd keep an eye out for it. Within a week, I was called for an interview.

My confidence was restored. With my 18 years of administrative experience, there wasn't much I didn't know or hadn't already done. I felt ready for the challenge ahead.

What was I thinking!?!

I was told during the interview process that once I worked for this CEO, I would be able to work for anyone. That should have been my first clue. Someone else warned me that the CEO was a perfectionist, and he would expect the same from his assistant. At that point, I explained to my interviewers that I considered myself a perfectionist as well, but that, as a human, I did occasionally make mistakes. However, I promised that I always learned from the experience so that it wouldn't happen again. Apparently, they were satisfied with that answer because they offered me the job. I went on to quickly prove that they had made the right decision.

Epilogue: My first mentor, Dick Clark, and I stayed in touch throughout the years, and he went on to have a very successful and rewarding career. At one point, he asked me to come work for him. I surprised myself by turning him down! I had matured a great deal, and the plain fact was that he could no longer afford me.

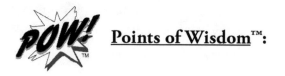 **Points of Wisdom™:**

- Seek out a mentor (an executive, a CEO, a CEO assistant) to advise you on what it takes to get to the CEO assistant level.
- Take control of your career by keeping abreast of new opportunities through formal and informal networks.
- If you don't hear back from a company you approach, have the courage to reach out to them again. You have nothing to lose!

TAKING "TEMP-TO-PERM" TO A WHOLE NEW LEVEL

Pam Shore, executive assistant to the CEO at Google, took "temp-to-perm" to a whole new level. Before she and Eric Schmidt moved to Google together, she assisted him "temporarily" at another company while he was actively seeking a permanent assistant. During his search, Pam decided to go for the job herself. Little did she know how much she still had to learn!

"Only those who will risk going too far can possibly find out how far one can go." – T.S. Eliot

One day, much to my surprise, the executive vice president and COO whom I had supported for five years announced her retirement, so I began interviewing for other positions within the company. Shortly thereafter, it was announced that Eric Schmidt would be joining the company as our new CEO.

As the only executive assistant without an executive to support, I became the obvious choice to help Eric get his office up and running and to assist him until he found his own executive assistant. What would happen to me after that was still a big question mark in my mind. I hoped something ideal would turn up while I was "temping" for Eric.

On the Friday afternoon before Eric officially started, I was rushing out of the office a few minutes before noon for a dental appointment. My phone rang, and as any good executive assistant would, I answered it. I wasn't happy about my overly developed sense of responsibility, however, because I knew the call would probably make me late for the dentist.

Thank goodness I did answer, though, because it was Eric. We exchanged pleasantries, and then he asked if I had a few minutes right then to go over the list of things that he needed done before Monday.

Gulp! "Eric, I'm sorry, but I actually don't have time right this minute. I cracked a tooth, and I'm on my way to the dentist to get it fixed. Would it be okay for me to call you back?"

He said it was fine, although I was sure he took it as a bad sign and would ask for someone else to temp for him. As I raced out the door, I thought to myself, "That's got to be the shortest job ever held as a CEO assistant."

When I did call Eric back hours later, I got his voicemail. I was actually relieved, since the Novocain made me practically incomprehensible. I didn't need to further tarnish his first impression of me by having a long conversation with what sounded like marbles in my mouth!

Monday came, and I began to work with Eric in person. He told me that he wanted to recruit the assistant he had left behind to work with him. (No surprise that he wanted me out of the job as soon as possible!) He asked the senior vice president of human resources and me to do whatever it took to convince her to make the move to come over with him. I extended an invitation to her to attend our all-hands meeting so she could meet us and see the company in action.

After the meeting, the three of us were walking back to Eric's office when Eric turned to me and asked, "So how did the meeting go? What did you think?"

That was a surprise. Rarely had I been asked for my opinion as to how an event was perceived by the employees. I was pleased that Eric cared enough to ask what I thought. Thank goodness I had been paying attention and was able to give him some constructive feedback! [Note to self: Always pay attention in meetings; you never know when you're going to be asked for your opinion.]

After two weeks, Eric's former assistant decided not to follow him to our company. In that time, I had become the most likely replacement, but I wasn't sure whether the position was right for me. Although I was enjoying working for Eric, and had supported many senior executives, I had never supported the *most* senior executive—the CEO. I wasn't sure that I could handle everything that the job entailed.

I discussed the situation with my husband, and we concluded that I had to give it a shot if it were offered; after all, I wouldn't know whether I could do it if I didn't try. I also didn't want to look back later and wonder what would have happened if I had taken this chance. (No risk; no reward.)

I sent Eric an email first thing the next morning, letting him know that I wanted to toss my hat into the ring to be his assistant. What a relief to learn that he welcomed the idea! When we met to discuss our potential working relationship, he confessed that since he had never been a CEO before, we would be learning this job together. I suggested that we give it six months; and if either of us changed our minds, we could part as friends. (That was 12 years ago.)

Once I was officially in the CEO assistant's position, I realized that I had been an armchair quarterback for years while I had supported the Number Two in command. I would silently criticize the CEO's assistant, wondering why she wasn't responding to my requests immediately. Didn't she see the urgency of the situations that I sent to her attention? I would think to myself, "If I were the CEO's assistant, I would be more on top of these things."

My, how your perspective changes once you're in the hot seat! When I ran into my predecessor several months later, I offered a humble apology for all my unspoken criticisms of her work, because I was sure that she had sensed them in my attitude towards her from time to time. I admitted to her that this job was not for the faint of heart.

Like her, I now understood that sometimes the lack of a response could actually yield better results than any response at all. Specifically, I recall a situation when a senior executive demanded that he be put in touch with Eric that instant. He claimed that it was critical to a large sales deal.

Eric had given me a heads-up the evening before that this request might occur. He told me that he didn't want to be involved so early in the negotiations. So I pushed back on the executive who called me, saying that I wouldn't be able to reach Eric for a few hours. I suggested that he get in touch with another senior executive to sort out the crisis.

He was not happy with my suggestion, but a few hours later when he checked back with me, the terms of the deal had changed for the better. Before I put him through to Eric, he told me that he had been able to get what he wanted from the other company. Later, Eric told me that he was pleased that the negotiations had gone favorably without his having to manage the process himself.

I still had so much more to learn. I discovered that coaching executives on how to work with the CEO was also part of my new job. This was not always comfortable for me, but I strove to rise to each occasion. I remember when an account representative handed me a PowerPoint presentation as the briefing package for Eric that was 45 pages long. This would never do. Knowing that Eric preferred something truly brief, I handed it back to the rep and suggested that he consolidate the materials into one page, with five major bullet points listing the goals of the meeting. I told him to include short biographies of all the attendees and any hot topics that might come up during the meeting.

The rep handed it right back to me in a huff. "Young lady," he said patronizingly, "I've been doing briefing packages for executives for 10 years, and this is how it is done."

Standing firm on my knowledge of Eric's preferences, I handed the package back to *him* one more time. I calmly explained that if he presented the information in the shorter format I had described, Eric was much more likely to review it. If he wanted to keep it as it was, the odds were that Eric would not open it before the meeting. I then picked up some other paperwork and turned back to my computer so he couldn't try to hand the package off to me again like some kind of "hot potato."

The account representative audibly gasped at what he perceived was my impertinent dismissal of him. I could feel another "Young lady" lecture about to erupt, so I threw him a bone. I turned back to him, gave him my biggest smile, and told him that he should feel free to use his current package as a detailed appendix to the one-page summary. No need for so much work to go to waste, I said. If the summary were intriguing enough, I added, Eric just might peruse the appendix. He just opened his mouth and then closed it again. Off he went with his feathers still ruffled to make the revisions that I had suggested.

I had won this round, and Eric told me later that it was the first time he had gotten a decent summary from that particular account representative. I chuckled to myself, knowing that my instincts had been right.

Just when I was beginning to feel comfortable in our partnership, Eric dropped a bomb on me. He had accepted the position of chairman of the board at Google. He remained chairman and CEO at our current company for a number of months, but his responsibilities at Google grew rapidly. I continued to try to support him at both companies. For a while, my desk became a plastic milk crate in my trunk, piled to the top with files that I transported back and forth between the two companies.

Ultimately, Eric resigned to become CEO at Google, in addition to his position as chairman there. But the biggest surprise was that he did not invite me to join him as his executive assistant at Google. My ego was bruised, but I knew Eric was actually trying to put what he thought were my best interests ahead of his own. Google's start-up environment would require long hours and a huge commitment, and he didn't want to impose that on me.

However, I missed our partnership. It took many heart-to-heart discussions with my husband before I finally approached Eric to let him know that I was interested in continuing our working relationship, if he was. He sounded pleased, and he invited me to attend some management meetings at Google so I could make up my own mind as to whether the move would be right for me.

I attended the meetings and assessed the pros and cons. It would mean a longer commute, a small start-up environment with little to no structure or processes in place, and a very young group of energetic folks – something that I was not accustomed to at the time. But the upside looked very bright: an opportunity to get in on the ground floor of a company that was clearly headed for big success. Again, I had the discussion with my husband, and we agreed that I had to give it a shot.

I was only the fourth assistant to join Google. The three assistants that were already on board were a great team. They taught me how to work with the engineers who truly ran the company. It was a new experience for me, and one that took some adjustment. Now, however, I can't imagine *not* being a part of the engineering world.

Eric consistently empowered me to promote changes that would be in the company's best interests and to improve the work environment wherever I saw the need. Early on at Google, I remember getting frustrated with the phone system, and one day I vented to Eric. He smiled and said, "Yes, I know it's a pain, but I also know you will figure out how to make it better." And with that, I was off to talk with facilities and telecom (okay, it was the same guy wearing two hats). I offered suggestions on how we needed to change the existing phone system to something that a larger company could use. Eight years later, I am proud to see that many processes and procedures like these, which I had a hand in putting in place, have taken root and grown with the company.

In many ways, it's been a wild ride as Eric's CEO assistant, but I'm still hanging on and having the time of my life.

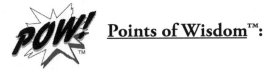 **Points of Wisdom™:**

- Be willing to take risks from time to time. No risk; no reward.
- Be assertive, but as diplomatic as possible, when coaching executives on how to get the best results from interactions with the CEO.

GO BACK TO YOUR DESK!

Linda McFarland offers a strategy for coping with stress. She adapted a slogan from a campy movie that helps her get and stay focused on the task at hand, no matter what else is going on. This mantra calms her down and enables her to get the most important things done. One day, though, her favorite slogan came back to bite her.

"In times of stress, be bold and valiant." – Horace

I have my own saying when I need to de-stress. It came from a movie called *Haiku Tunnel* about a neurotic male secretary, Josh, who was a terrific temp, but became a nervous wreck whenever he was made a permanent employee.

One scene really hit home for me. Near the end of the movie, Josh was having a very bad day at work. He became overwhelmed with the number of things that were going wrong and felt like a complete and utter failure. Finally, he went into his executive's office and had a major meltdown. The executive briefly looked up from his work and calmly said, "Josh, go back to your desk. Settle down. Focus. And catch up."

Those words triggered an epiphany for me. I have used them on myself a number of times, with a slight tweak. Whenever I'm close to the edge of my own nervous breakdown and can't focus, I say to myself (often out loud): "Linda, go back to your desk. Settle down. Focus. And GET IT DONE!" I've added emphatic hand gestures, which I think help immensely.

One time my favorite phrase came back to bite me. Our company was rolling out their mandatory online sexual harassment training program. The deadline to complete the training was fast approaching, and I realized that the CEO hadn't done it yet. Now wasn't *that* being a great role model for the rest of the company? How would it look if the CEO showed up on the non-compliant list?

I decided to take action to make him get it done. I blocked out an appointment on his calendar, and when the time arrived, I walked into his office to launch the online application on his computer. I wasn't fast enough. The CEO acted like a cat who knew I was about to take him to the vet for his annual shots. Before I could try to block him, he was out of his chair and through the door. (This was typical behavior for him when too many things were demanding his attention.)

"Where are you going?" I called out. He mumbled about having to check something with another executive and disappeared. I finished bringing the application up on his monitor and went back to my desk to await his eventual return. I figured that he couldn't escape me forever.

When he reappeared an hour later, I said, "I've logged you into the training and you're running out of time." But I could tell that he wasn't really listening. Within minutes, he took off to see another executive about some other "pressing" matter.

In his absence, I became caught up in my own workload. It was a busy day, and I had a long travel itinerary to finish for him. After 30 minutes, I became restless and found that I could not focus on the itinerary until I knew the CEO was back in his office, sitting in front of the computer, clicking away with the online training.

Finally, he reappeared. I jumped to my feet, exclaiming, "You're running out of time to complete the harassment training. It's time for you to go back to your desk, settle down, focus, and GET IT DONE!"

Of course, I included my hand gestures just to make sure that I was absolutely clear.

He had heard me say this out loud to myself countless times. He chuckled at the fact that I was using it on him, but it had the effect I wanted. With a sheepish grin, he went into his office and finally obeyed.

About 45 minutes later, his door burst open. The CEO came bounding out with a smile on his face that stretched from ear to ear. "I finished the training!" he boasted, as he continued down the hall. (As if he ever would have done it on his own.)

I thought it was funny when he started poking his head through the doors of the other executives who hadn't yet completed their training. "I'm done with my harassment training; what about you?" He kept up the inquiries all the way down the hall until he disappeared around the corner. What a relief that my "go-back-to-your-desk" mantra had worked on him!

I soon became engrossed in putting the final details together for his upcoming trip. My stress level began to rise as a few missing parts simply refused to come together. It also didn't help that other members of the management team kept interrupting me about various matters. Couldn't they see that I was busy?

The CEO passed by me again on his way back into his office. He had completed his training on time, had bragged about it to a sufficient number of subordinates, felt very pleased with himself, and was ready to go home.

He called me into his office. "Linda, I'm ready to leave; where's my trip itinerary?"

"It's not quite ready," I replied, with an audible note of stress in my voice.

Without hesitation, he stood up. Using the same hand gestures I had used on him just a couple of hours earlier, he commanded, "Linda, go back to your desk, settle down, focus, and GET IT DONE!"

I was speechless. How dare he use my own mantra against me! Who did he think he was?

Then I noticed that he was struggling to keep the corners of his mouth from curling up. He was loving this. Without being able to help myself, I burst out laughing, and he busted up, too. The tension was broken.

When I had managed to stop giggling long enough to shoot one more comeback at him, I said in my haughtiest tone: "I'll get your itinerary to you in the same amount of time it took you to do your sexual harassment training." I turned on my heel and walked out of his office before he could think of a retort, and before I broke out laughing again.

 <u>**Points of Wisdom**</u>™:

- Don't be afraid to use humor with your executive, especially when you need to follow up with him about something that he'd rather not do.
- Have a mantra that you can repeat over and over when it seems as though there is just too much work. Ideally, your mantra will calm you down, help you focus, and enable you to get the important things done.

GREAT EXPECTATIONS

Joanne Linden thought she was ready to take on a demanding CEO, but she began to wonder if his expectations of her were too great.

"I long to accomplish a great and noble task; but it is my chief duty to accomplish small tasks as if they were great and noble."
– Helen Keller

To say that working for this CEO was an intense experience would be putting it mildly. Not only did he require brilliant work from all his direct reports, but my transition from a vice president's assistant to a CEO's assistant presented additional daily challenges. While the interpersonal skills that I had honed over the years served me well in acclimating to the new company culture and the personalities of everyone below the CEO, I had to stretch to the *nth* degree to meet his expectations.

For example, in the past, if someone had requested time on my executive's calendar, I scheduled the meeting with no questions asked. It was an unspoken rule that if someone asked to meet with your executive, there must be a good reason for it. Who was I to question another VP or a director as to why he or she needed to have a meeting with my VP?

Not so with my new CEO! Scheduling meetings for a CEO is a different ball game altogether. The first time I reviewed the CEO's upcoming calendar with him during our one-on-one session, he asked me why I had scheduled him to meet with the VP of corporate communications, who wasn't one of his direct reports. Why wasn't the VP of corporate communications meeting with the senior vice president of marketing, who could then meet with the CEO and tell him whatever he needed to know about corporate communications?

My response was simple: "Because the VP of corporate communications requested the meeting." Needless to say, that was not the answer my CEO was looking for. He wanted to know the subject of the meeting, why he wasn't meeting with the senior VP of marketing, who else was going to be in the meeting, and what, if anything, he needed to do to prepare for the meeting.

Whew! That was a tall order, and the CEO expected that kind of briefing for every single meeting on his calendar. How unreasonable was that?

Over time, I discovered that the CEO had good reason to question all the meetings requested of him. I learned that many people would bypass proper channels if they could get away with it. They figured that if they could just get face time with the CEO and obtain his buy-in, they would have saved themselves and the company a lot of time. In reality, they slowed down the entire process by attempting this, because the CEO would not authorize anything until all the proper channels had been consulted. Therefore, instead of saving time, they had just added one more step.

Aside from the players and the meeting content, there was even more for me to learn in terms of the protocol involved in scheduling the meeting location. In my previous positions, whenever someone who outranked my executive requested a meeting, it always took place in the higher-ranking person's office. I thought this was an unwritten rule that everyone obeyed. So when the chairman of the board of a company on which my CEO served as a board member requested a meeting with him, I naively assumed that the meeting would take place at the chairman's company. Did I bother to check out my assumption? It never even occurred to me.

Imagine my embarrassment when the meeting time arrived, and I received a call from our lobby, announcing that the chairman was here for his meeting with my CEO. Of course, my CEO was already en route to the chairman's company for the meeting. Oops!

Unfortunately, this was long before cell phones, so there was no way to reach my CEO until he arrived at his destination. I had to call the chairman's assistant with my tail between my legs and ask her to have my CEO turn around as soon as he arrived there and come all the way back to our company.

You can be sure that I never made *that* mistake again. To this day, whenever I schedule a meeting for my CEO, I always confirm not only the day and the time, but also the place.

If only calendaring were all I had to learn. Travel for a CEO was a whole new dimension for me. None of my former executives had done much traveling. When they did, I simply made the reservations and handed them their ticket and the itinerary provided by the travel agency.

This CEO had an entirely different set of expectations. He traveled extensively and demanded minute-by-minute instructions, down to exactly where in the airport his driver would meet him. Have you ever tried to specify a particular landmark in a terminal as vast as New York's John F. Kennedy Airport? Let me tell you, it's not my idea of fun.

But the level of detail required could be even worse than that. If he were going to be in New York City and would be walking from his hotel to a meeting, which way should he turn on the street when he walked out the lobby door—right or left? North or south? East or west? (Did he think I was a compass?) How long would it take him to walk to his meeting location? I almost needed to visit his travel destinations before he got there, just to pace out the steps and include those numbers in his itinerary.

I learned what the CEO's favorite hotel in New York was—even his favorite room in that hotel. There were never any loose ends in his travel itinerary; it was precise down to the last detail. Spontaneity while traveling on business was not his cup of tea.

But traveling to see customers was only half the story. When the CEO interacted with customers from the comfort of his own office, there were new procedures for me to learn as well.

Customers are the life blood of any company. Therefore, I assumed that if a customer called the CEO, I should pass the call to him immediately, right?

Wrong! The last thing any CEO wants is to appear clueless about the situation that a customer is calling about. The CEO patiently explained to me that I should politely tell the customer that he was not available at the moment, and that I would have him return the call as soon as possible. Then, before even talking to the CEO, I should apprise the sales department of the customer's call and ask them for a briefing on any relevant issues before the CEO returned the customer's call. (There's a reason that CEOs appear to be so in control of their worlds. It's that we executive assistants control that world *for* them.)

Learning to be the assistant to the CEO sometimes felt like a trial by fire. I discovered the hard way that small talk can be just another form of interrogation, whether it is an employee coming by my cubicle "just to say hi" or an investment analyst calling the CEO's office to try to nose out the upcoming end-of-quarter results. The most innocent response to a mundane question can easily be misconstrued and come back to haunt you.

For example, on the last day of the quarter, an analyst might call the CEO's office and ask to speak to him. Of course, the CEO would not be available, so the analyst would talk to me: "How's it going over there? Is it crazy?"

My response of either "Yeah, it's crazy" or "No, it's not bad" could be interpreted to mean that, in the first case, my company was scrambling to close orders, or worse, in the latter case, there were no orders coming in on the last day of the quarter. Bad news either way.

The "Buy" or "Sell" advice would show up in the analyst's published predictions the next day, based on what I had thought was only idle chit-chat. The first time this happened, my face was beet red. Who knew I was so important that I could be the source for an analyst's recommendation? Analysts could not be trusted under any circumstances. The best answer to a seemingly idle question was always a smooth evasion. I had to be on my toes every second.

All in all, the company's recruiter had been right: Once I had worked for their CEO, I could work for *any* CEO. After working with him for seven years, the company was acquired by a larger company, and I moved on to my next CEO, Aart de Geus at Synopsys. I thought I was definitely prepared and ready for anything now...*or was I?*

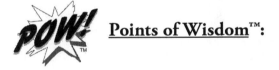 **Points of Wisdom™:**

- Manage your boss's world; at his level, he no longer has time to manage you.
- Be proud of your chosen profession. In many ways, you truly do run the company.
- What you consider to be minor details, your CEO considers vital information because it eliminates ambiguity and makes his life easier.
- You must be on your toes at all times; don't take anything, even idle small talk, at face value.

PANIC ROOM

When Cisco built a few secure storage rooms onsite, Debbie Gross, chief executive assistant to the CEO, went to inspect hers. She was horrified to see the actual size of the room. Debbie is very claustrophobic, and this room definitely pushed her panic button.

"Panic is a sudden desertion of us, and a going over to the enemy of our imagination." – Christian Nevell Bovee

Like many companies, Cisco has storage rooms designed to keep important documents secure and confidential. When our first secure storage room was ready for use, I went over to inspect it. In order to get in and out of the room, I had to use special keys for multiple locks. I was finally able to get all the deadbolts unlocked, and I stepped inside the room.

I let out a loud gasp. They certainly hadn't splurged on space! The room was so tiny that I couldn't imagine how our files would fit inside it. As I stood there in complete shock at the size of the storage room, claustrophobia set in. I made a vow then and there: I would place or retrieve files in that room only if I kept the door wide open while I was inside.

One day John Chambers, Cisco's CEO, asked me to go with him to retrieve a very confidential file that we had placed in the secure storage room. Once I had unlocked the multiple locks and opened the door, John stepped inside. I hesitated as I stood outside the storage room. John said, "Come on in; I need your help to find that file."

Much to my dismay, I realized that I was going to have to step inside that extremely tiny room with my boss still in there to help search for the file. There was barely room for one of us in there, much less two. John seemed to sense my hesitation, I thought, and looked at me with a question in his eyes. I imagined he was thinking, "What's taking her so long?" So I took a deep breath and stepped inside.

Once inside, I moved to one side of the tiny space so he could reach the top box of files. In moving aside, I had to let go of the door. It slammed shut. I reached for the handle of the door only to find that it would not open. I yanked on it several times with no results. I was about to scream for help when I remembered that the storage room had been retrofitted and the walls were solid—I mean solid—concrete!

By now, my face was flushed and my heart was beating rapidly. This felt like a horror movie. John suddenly realized how uncomfortable I was and began to laugh. "You mean to tell me we are both locked in here?" he chuckled.

John suggested that I use my cell phone. I would have been happy to—if it weren't still sitting on my desk! I could have died from complete embarrassment.

Still chuckling, John had the presence of mind to try the door himself. He went over and gave it a good shove. Magically, it opened. I practically tripped over John to bolt out the door before he could get out of the way. I could still hear him laughing behind me as I flew down the hallway.

My motto since then: "Always take an understanding buddy (not your boss) to stand at the door for you when you have to go into the secure storage room!"

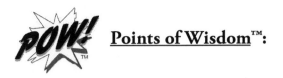 **<u>Points of Wisdom</u>™:**

- When you're in a tight spot, keep calm. Laughing will ease the tension.
- Even in stressful situations, if you remain calm, you will think of solutions to try. One of them will work.
- Display a calm attitude in moments of stress; it will calm others so much that they may even forget you're in the middle of a crisis.

MISSING IN ACTION

What began as a ski trip with friends soon turned into a horror story, but only the CEO's assistant, Linda McFarland, suspected that all was not well. Refusing to ignore her instincts, she persisted in tracking down the CEO's movements throughout the weekend until she succeeded in getting a search-and-rescue team to try to find him in a deadly blizzard.

"Trust your instinct to the end, though you can render no reason." – Ralph Waldo Emerson

It was almost a week before Christmas. Several coworkers and I were preparing for a holiday potluck luncheon. Our CEO had joined the festivities and sat down to eat at our table. He had recently relocated to Silicon Valley from Chicago. As we all discussed our plans for the holidays, he shared with us that his family was going to celebrate the holidays at their Florida home. He had some things to wrap up at the office the following week, so they had gone ahead of him, and he would follow them as soon as he could.

As a ski enthusiast, our CEO wanted to get in a weekend of skiing with some buddies before his last week in the office. The coming weekend, with his family away, was a perfect time. He had arranged to meet some friends at Lake Tahoe that evening. Although it looked as though a bad storm was heading our way, he had committed to the trip. A little bad weather wasn't going to stop him. After all, it was his last chance to ski before spending a snow-free Christmas in Florida.

At the end of the day, as he dashed out the door, I asked him for the name of his hotel. He said if there was anything urgent, just to call him on his cell. He said I didn't have to be in charge of his vacation. Then off he went for his weekend in the snow.

I kept hearing about the horrible weather in Tahoe all weekend—one of the worst "white-out" storms in years. Not only were the roads closed, but most of the resorts were shut down, too. I remember thinking that I bet he wished he had waited until after Christmas to go there. Because of the weather, he probably wasn't even going to get a chance to ski. Then I remembered how busy Monday's calendar was and hoped he didn't get snowed in.

I arrived at the office on Monday at 8:15 a.m. The CEO's office was dark. That was unusual; he typically arrived by 7 a.m. If he was going to be late, he always called or emailed me. Had he gotten snowed in after all? Was he sleeping in front of a roaring fire somewhere in Tahoe while I was getting ready to put in a long day at work? *Lucky bum!*

I checked my voicemail. No message. I called his cell. No answer. I tried his home. No answer. I checked email. Nothing.

This was not normal behavior for him. I had a feeling something was wrong, so I didn't waste any time. My gut told me to take action.

I recalled the brief conversation I had had with him the previous Friday. I knew that he was meeting friends in Tahoe and remembered the name of one of his friends, "Sam." When I called Sam, he picked right up.

I asked Sam if he had connected with our CEO over the weekend. "Nope," he said. The roads were bad, and he had arrived late Saturday morning to find that our CEO had already checked in. Sam had assumed he was on the slopes. Sam wasn't aware if he had connected with any of their other friends, so he made an attempt to find him. He had tried my boss's cell, but there had been no answer. He had even called the Highway Patrol to ask about accidents, but nothing had been reported.

Sam stayed the night at the hotel, but when the CEO never returned, Sam figured he had made other plans, and he left for home.

I couldn't believe what I had heard. I asked Sam very calmly if he had called the hotel back later to see if our CEO had ever returned. Suddenly, Sam realized the gravity of the situation. He was speechless. I asked for the hotel number so I could call. Sam insisted that he would make the call himself. Perhaps guilt had kicked in, or else he was just worried.

While I waited for news, I felt worse and worse. I remembered the weather forecast. Tahoe had been in a "white-out" storm for two-and-a-half days. Our CEO could be out there somewhere with only his ski gear. How would he survive?

Sam called back within minutes. I heard concern in his voice. The CEO had never returned to the hotel. In fact, the hotel had moved all of his things out of the empty room to their luggage storage area.

Since Sam was a good friend of the family, he agreed to make the call to the CEO's wife. Boy, was I glad that *he,* not I, was going to make that call.

But I couldn't just sit and wait to hear back from Sam; I wanted to help. So, while Sam made the call, I started my list of next steps. I would call the ski resorts in the area. Maybe I'd get lucky and they would find his car in one of the parking lots. I also thought it would help to pinpoint when the CEO went missing by checking his bank account and credit cards.

I was feeling pretty helpless. If only I had kept a list of his important information, including his car's license plate number. It was unlikely that his wife would have this number with her, since the family was now at their Florida vacation home. I knew I would be hard pressed to come up with my license plate number in an emergency. I crossed my fingers and added "call car insurance" to the list, hoping I could get the license plate number from them.

By this time, I was wishing I had a crystal ball. *Where was he?* How was I going to tell the executive staff that our CEO was missing in action? I looked at the time and realized that it was already 9:45 a.m. His weekly staff meeting was scheduled to begin in 15 minutes.

It was time to update the CFO, who was second in command. I gave him all the information that I had. He looked at me with disbelief. This kind of thing happened only in the movies.

After recovering from his initial horror, the CFO tried to reassure me by complimenting me on my calm attitude and ability to focus on what needed to be done. He said that I was making good progress in a difficult situation.

But none of that mattered to me. I just wanted someone to find our CEO. We talked about what the CFO should tell the staff. He prepared a brief statement, and I went back to my detective work. We agreed that I would provide him with updates as soon as I had any new information.

As I returned to my desk, the phone was ringing. It was the CEO's wife. By now, the news had begun to sink in, and I realized it was going to be difficult to have a productive conversation. To get us both focused on achieving a positive outcome, I reviewed my list of next steps with her. We briefly talked about ways to get the license number of the car and to check to see if he had used his credit cards. That would help us pinpoint a time when he went missing. She agreed to tackle those tasks. I told her I would start contacting ski resorts to see if his car was in anyone's parking lot. Since we didn't have his license number, we'd have to go with a description of the car.

I left messages with the security departments at several ski resorts. Finally, a call back came from one of them. Bad news. Every night, all remaining cars in the parking lot were towed. It was their policy. The security guard that called me back suggested I call Search and Rescue to see if they could help. About that same time, Sam called.

42

He had made some good progress. The hotel had our CEO's license number for the car. Luckily, he had written it on the hotel registration form. A call was placed to the Highway Patrol, and we learned that the car had been towed from Squaw Valley. Finally, a real clue! Now it was time to call Search and Rescue. We had a location to begin the search.

By now it was almost 11 a.m. on Monday. No one had seen our CEO since Saturday morning.

I provided Search and Rescue with the information we had about our missing CEO. I was hoping we had enough details to get a search underway. My gut kept screaming the urgency of the situation. They were willing to help, but they wanted to confirm a few details with the CEO's wife. After that, finally, a unit was dispatched. I kept thinking, "Is this really happening? This has to be a horrible dream."

The hours seemed to crawl by.

About 1:15 p.m., I received a call. Our CEO was alive and safe. The Search and Rescue helicopter had located him in the snow. I sent up a silent prayer of gratitude.

Eventually, I learned what had happened. Our CEO had been skiing his way down the mountain when the storm had grown too thick to see. The weather had changed in a matter of minutes. He had never skied at Squaw Valley before, and somehow he had gotten off the marked path. Even if there had been a path down the mountain, the storm was so bad that he could barely see a few feet in front of him. Using his survival skills as a former Marine, he had taken cover and managed to make it through the storm.

He had been missing for over 48 hours. Although he was exhausted and suffered some frostbite, he was alive.

I kept hoping I would have an opportunity to talk to him then, but that didn't happen. I was glad that at least he was safe and in the hands of good doctors. I received updates about his progress throughout the evening. The media even covered the story during the evening news. I was exhausted after this incredible ordeal.

The next day I arrived at work at the usual time. Around noon, I finally received a call from our CEO. What a relief to hear his voice! We talked briefly about the team effort it had taken to find him.

Then he said, "Linda, thanks for not waiting until the afternoon to look for me. I don't think I would have made it." He thanked me several times for taking action to save his life. I couldn't think of anything to say except, "You're welcome. I'm so glad you're okay."

Trusting my instincts helped give this story a happy ending. Although it took a team effort to save our CEO, I had felt that it was my responsibility to get things moving because *"I had a feeling..."* I learned more than ever the importance of trusting my gut.

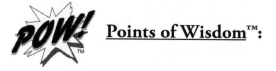 **Points of Wisdom™**:

- Be committed and resilient, even when everything goes wrong.
- Always pay attention, even if the conversation sounds casual or unimportant, so you will be able to recall what you heard later. Those details might mean the difference between life and death.
- It is crucial to know your executive's usual habits so you can tell when something isn't right.
- In some situations, you need to take action, figure out next steps, and develop a plan even when you don't have all the information that you think you need.

PLANES, TRAINS, AND HANDLING CHANGE

Bonnie Savage had to use good judgment when her CEO's flight was rerouted.

"Don't be afraid to give your best to what seemingly are small jobs. Every time you conquer one, it makes you that much stronger. If you do the little jobs well, the big ones tend to take care of themselves." – Dale Carnegie

While working as the CEO assistant to Beatriz Infante, I was preparing to leave the office one day when she was away on one of her many trips to the East Coast. Beatriz was returning that evening specifically to attend an important family event. I always made it a habit to check the flight-tracking website to verify her arrival time. It made my evening more relaxing to know that everything was on schedule, especially this evening, as I had dinner plans with my own family.

As I looked on the website, I was concerned to see that the flight was traveling off course. Without delay I got on the phone with the airline. I had a sinking feeling that my own evening was going to be delayed. To my dismay, I learned that Beatriz's flight had been rerouted due to bad weather.

As result of the rerouting, it was evident that Beatriz would miss her connecting flight. Since she and I had no way to communicate, I knew I had to take immediate action on her behalf, using my own best judgment.

Given that it was already after hours, I worked with our back-up travel agent. After talking through the options, we decided to try another flight connection departing a little later. Thank goodness we were able to secure the very last seat.

Knowing that I would be out to dinner with my family when her plane finally landed, I took the final flight details with me to dinner. When her plane landed, I was sure that she would call me first, and she did.

When I saw her call, I picked up with the details in hand and began to explain the alternate plan that I had already put in place. I had long ago trained my family to be quiet when I was talking to my boss; they knew I was on call 24/7 and treated the situation as they would a doctor on call. My husband just hoped I wouldn't have to cut our dinner short. Fortunately, that wasn't the case this night.

Beatriz was relieved to learn that I was already aware of the situation and had been proactive in making changes to her flight reservation and car service. She was happy with all my decisions, and I was able to go back to dinner with my family. She arrived home in time for her own family event—and I ended up with a great reference for life.

 **Points of Wisdom™:**

- Be proactive whenever your executive travels. You never know when there may be changes in the weather or mechanical problems with the plane.
- Empower yourself to make decisions when you are unable to communicate with your executive.
- Be prepared with information to assist your executive 24/7, even if it means carting details around with you on your personal time.

- Make sure your family and friends understand that you have the kind of job where you could be called away at a moment's notice to attend to your boss's needs.

BLACKOUT IN NEW YORK

Linda McFarland details how she maneuvered her CEO through New York during the 2003 Northeastern blackout.

"Accept challenges so that you may feel the exhilaration of victory." – George S. Patton

Have you ever been thrust into a situation so challenging that you wished you could just wave a magic wand to fix it? How much easier that would be than doing all the work to actually solve the problem, especially when it seems to have infinite facets.

I've found that when things go wrong, it isn't productive to argue with your executive. What matters is solving the problem before anyone has a meltdown. A magic wand would certainly come in handy at those times. But contrary to our CEO's beliefs about us, we are just not equipped with that much-needed office accessory. Instead, what we have are our networks, our creativity, and most importantly, our brains.

Time after time, assistants are thrown into crisis situations and expected to make snap decisions without wavering. Even without a magic wand, most assistants are remarkably capable of handling the unexpected. You know you have made the grade as a CEO assistant when your executive goes from questioning your advice to following your instructions to the letter.

In one situation, I had been working with Jeff Rodek, the chairman and CEO of Hyperion, for about three years. In the summer of 2003,

I put together an intense week of back-to-back meetings for him with investors and financial analysts in New York.

Once they were on the road, Jeff and our director of investor relations checked in with me periodically. The meetings were going well, they reported, but were very wearing. Jeff had to deliver the same message over and over without showing any signs of fatigue; in fact, he had to appear enthusiastic every time. Finally, they finished and were headed for LaGuardia Airport.

Whenever Jeff travels, if he knows he's going to get to the airport sooner than expected, he always calls me to check on earlier flights. (Patience probably isn't his strong suit.) Knowing him as I did, I was ready when he called this time. I had a dozen earlier departures for him to choose from. However, I warned him that if we changed his flights, he would lose his upgrade to first class.

There was a slight pause while he weighed comfort versus speed. Although he didn't want to admit it, he was beat. Comfort won out. He told me to stick with the original plan.

Just before he hung up the phone, he mentioned that his cell phone battery was running low. "Did you bring your spare battery?" I asked. When he mumbled some excuse, I let it go. No sense lecturing him again, I thought to myself. I simply told him that I would be on my cell phone if he needed to reach me. Since his plans were settled, I was going to run down the street to grab a sandwich.

It was about 1 p.m. my time on Thursday, August 14, 2003.

Less than 15 minutes after I left, my cell phone rang. It was Jeff already. I crossed my fingers, hoping that he hadn't decided to change flights after all. I didn't have my notes on the other flights with me at the sandwich shop.

However, that wasn't the problem. His voice sounded agitated, so I asked him if anything was wrong. He said, "The lights and electricity are out in the airport. I called my wife to turn on the TV for news about the situation, and there are blackouts throughout New York and Connecticut."

We both had the same immediate fear: Was it a terrorist attack? Two years after 9/11, whenever anything went wrong with the country's infrastructure, the possibility of a terrorist attack was still uppermost in everyone's minds. (Fortunately, we later found out that that wasn't the case. It was a simple but widespread electrical failure, but we didn't know that during our conversation.)

Jeff asked, "Linda, have you ever seen a movie where people go hysterical in an airport?"

"Yes," I replied cautiously.

"This situation is worse than anything I've ever seen in the movies," he shrieked. "Get me outta here now!"

In Jeff's usual form, he started barking orders like a drill sergeant. Even after three years, his impulse was to give me instructions before asking for my suggestions. I took a deep breath and asked him whether he had the tiny travel flashlight I had given him to carry on trips. After all, he was in the midst of a blackout. When I was met with dead silence, I had my answer. (Don't lecture, don't lecture, I told myself sternly.)

Jeff was calling from a phone booth since his cell phone battery was low, but he still had a few minutes of talk time left on his cell; we just didn't know how many. Since Jeff didn't want to lose communication with me until we had a solid plan, we agreed on a system: I would put him on hold on his pay phone, start making calls, and come back to him between my calls to give him updates. This meant that he would have to be patient and trust me while he was on hold, and that's the part that worried me.

My first instinct was to call our travel agent. But with a twinge in my gut, I remembered that she was on vacation. I placed a call and hoped the back-up travel agent could help me, even though he was new and inexperienced.

I explained the situation carefully and then proceeded to bombard him with instructions. (Maybe Jeff and I had something in common after all?) "I need you to secure a rental car at LaGuardia Airport, check on flights departing from other New York airports, and look for a hotel with its own generator and, if possible, a restaurant onsite." I heard the agent's sharp intake of breath in reaction to my demands just before I put him on hold, and I went back to Jeff to update him.

Just as I had feared, Jeff's mind had raced elsewhere in the meantime. What was happening to our office in Connecticut? Were the lights out there, too? Were our employees safe? Was our data secure? I told Jeff that would be my next call.

I tried several numbers for our Connecticut office, but no one answered. (Not a good sign.) As a last resort, I tried the front desk. To my relief, the receptionist picked up. I told her quickly about Jeff and asked her about conditions at the office and in that general area.

The receptionist told me that they had lost power, too, and all the employees had been sent home. She was just walking out the door when I called. Luckily, she hadn't ignored the ringing phone.

I asked her if our back-up generator was working. She assured me that it had started immediately, and IT had confirmed that all our data was safe and secure.

It was a relief to hear her next question. "Is there anything I can do for you or Jeff? I'd be happy to stay longer if you need some help." What a stroke of luck! Although I worked on the West Coast, I had many opportunities to interact with this receptionist on the East Coast over the years. We had developed a friendly rapport, and now that relationship was paying off. She took over finding Jeff a limo, and we agreed that the smartest plan was to send him to Connecticut, away from the mob scene in New York.

I put the call on hold and picked up the other line where Jeff was still holding. I quickly gave him an update. He was relieved to know that our Connecticut office was in good shape, but he was getting impatient again. He felt useless standing in a phone booth. "Call me on my cell for any updates," he said. "I'm getting in line for a rental car."

Was he crazy? I had already told him that we were arranging a car for him. But that was Jeff. (Don't argue with him, I told myself.) I felt a headache coming on. I said a quick prayer and hoped that when I tried his cell phone later, it would still be working.

When I picked up the phone to talk to the receptionist, she filled me in on her progress. She had found a sedan available near the airport, and the driver was heading Jeff's way. She needed to provide the driver with a destination after the pick-up. So I called the travel agent to find out if he had come up with a hotel option.

What luck! He had secured two reservations online at a hotel in Connecticut. Even better, it had a generator *and* a restaurant. But there was a catch. The hotel's computer and fax were both down, and we needed their confirmation number to make sure they would honor the reservation. The phone lines from the West Coast were all jammed. Neither the travel agent nor I could get through to them.

I had to think fast. I went back to our receptionist, who was still holding from our Connecticut office. Could she try to call the hotel for the confirmation number since it was a local call for her? She agreed and quickly came back to me with good news. She had gotten through. Jeff was confirmed and I had confirmation numbers for him and our director of investor relations.

I called Jeff to give him the good news, hoping that there were enough minutes left on his cell phone to be able to receive it. When he picked up, I blurted out in a rush, "We found a limo driver and he's headed your way. Meet him at the usual spot. He'll be holding a sign with your name. And we've got a hotel for you in Connecticut that has power and a working restaurant onsite."

To my surprise, Jeff sounded irritated. "But I told you I was going to be in line for a rental car. There are only a few people in front of me now."

I took a deep breath before I answered, trying to hide my disappointment at his lack of appreciation. The best strategy was to appeal to his logic. "Okay, if you want to take your chances with a rental car, that's fine with me. But don't forget you can't pump gas without electricity. In fact, with the computers down, who knows how long it will take to complete the paperwork to rent the car?"

Reluctantly, Jeff agreed to go to the pick-up area for the limo that our receptionist had arranged. I gave him a quick update regarding the hotel, and I asked him to call me once he was in the limo.

When Jeff and the director of investor relations arrived at the pick-up area, they had to fight through a mob to reach the limo. As the two of them approached the driver, they could see other people offering the driver money to take them instead. Fortunately, the driver had waited for Jeff. Later, our director told me that as they were driving away, she had experienced an almost surreal feeling at leaving the chaos at the airport behind. What a relief to be on their way to Connecticut!

I called the travel agent back. We had to look ahead to the next steps. What flights were available from Connecticut? This time, he was ahead of me; he was already holding a flight for the next morning from Newark. Way to go! Before I could thank him, my phone rang again. It was Jeff.

Jeff was still in complaint mode. He didn't understand why I had booked him a hotel room in Connecticut instead of New York, and he wanted me to check departing flights for this evening again, just in case

I had missed something. I screamed silently to myself. Enough already! Was there no way to please this man?

I had access to the Internet, and I could see mobs of people flooding the streets of New York. I told Jeff what I was looking at online. I said, "Jeff, if you want to go back to New York and fight the crowds to find a hotel that has a generator and a restaurant, you go for it." I also reminded him that it would be safer and more logical to have him near our Connecticut office. After a long moment, Jeff agreed to continue on to Connecticut. I hung up just as my other line rang.

I was so excited to hear the caller's voice. It was our regular travel agent, who was still on vacation. She had heard the news about the blackout, remembered planning Jeff's trip with me, and called in from her vacation just to see if I needed any help. What a pal! Because Jeff traveled constantly, we had developed a genuine friendship over the years. Jeff was safely on his way to Connecticut, the next day's flights were set, and I finally had a chance to look up. All the work that I had planned to get done that day was still sitting there from the night before. What a joke! I picked up the first piece of paper and dug in.

At 6 p.m., Jeff called to check in. It was 9 p.m. where he was, and he had arrived at the hotel and eaten dinner. He told me that the hallways had lighting, but the rooms didn't have electricity.

I couldn't resist saying, "If only you had brought your travel flashlight." (Now that didn't count as a lecture, did it?) For now, he was going to have to use candles.

I gave him an update regarding plans for the next morning. I also suggested that he might want to plug in his cell phone to recharge, just in case the electricity came on during the night. Before we hung up, Jeff grudgingly admitted, "Well, I guess it's better to be here than at the airport." (Was that a thank-you? Be still, my heart! It was the closest thing I was going to get to one that night.)

Jeff met the driver early the next morning and made it to the Newark airport in time for his flight. Just before getting on the plane, he picked up a newspaper.

Jeff called me as soon as he landed. He had read the articles about the blackout during his flight home and realized the gravity of the situation that I had steered him out of. "How did you get me out of that airport?" Jeff asked with something close to incredulity in his voice. "Thank you."

This was the thanks I had been waiting for. I knew I had pulled the proverbial rabbit out of the hat for him, even if he didn't spell it out. Who needs a magic wand when you've got brains, networks, and creativity? But the best part of all was that Jeff didn't question my travel instructions again for at least a month.

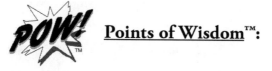 **Points of Wisdom™:**

- There is always a solution to any problem, no matter how difficult the situation.
- If you don't panic, the details are more likely to fall into place.
- Train your CEO to rely on *you* to be the logistics manager.
- Don't lecture your CEO when he's in the midst of a messy situation; you can always do a post mortem later when you are both calmer.
- Develop a network with vendors and colleagues that you can count on in a crisis.

TWO SHIPS PASSING
IN THE NIGHT

Joanne Linden leveraged her relationship with another CEO assistant and her knowledge of the other CEO's personal circumstances—along with a little luck—to make an "impossible" meeting take place, with lucrative results.

"Apply yourself…do something. Don't just stand there; make it happen." – Lee Iacocca

Good relationships with assistants to CEOs of other companies can be an invaluable resource. Whenever you have the opportunity, take the time to develop them. I know we often feel we're too busy to make time for small talk, but over the years, lots of information gets shared; and you just never know when one of those tidbits of information is going to pay off.

One afternoon during the last week of the quarter, I received a frantic phone call from a Synopsys salesman. He asked me to schedule a phone call between my CEO, Aart, and the CEO of one of our biggest customers – *today*!

My first reaction was, "No way, it's impossible." Aart was leaving for the airport in an hour; he didn't have time. However, I also knew that this phone call could mean the difference between making our quarterly financial projections or not, and Wall Street would be very unforgiving if we didn't.

I didn't need to check with Aart. I knew what he would want me to do.

Fortunately, I had a long-standing working relationship with Nancy, the CEO's assistant at the other company. I picked up the phone and prepared to ask for the impossible. When I explained the situation and asked if the two CEOs could speak now, Nancy truly wanted to help me because I had always been helpful to her. But not surprisingly, she had to say, "I'm sorry, but he's on his way to the airport shortly and can't speak right now." CEOs' calendars don't usually allow for last-minute requests.

Still scrambling for a solution, my next thought was to suggest that they have the phone conversation while they were both driving to the airport. But suddenly, a different idea occurred to me. Those years of relationship-building had paid off, as I remembered Nancy telling me that her boss worked in the San Francisco Bay Area, but lived out of California in the same city where Aart happened to be flying!

I asked Nancy if her CEO was, by chance, flying home. She confirmed that he was. I then asked what flight he was on. By sheer luck, Aart was on exactly the same flight.

Knowing that a face-to-face meeting would be far better than a phone conversation, I suggested that the two CEOs meet at the airport while waiting for their flight. Nancy quickly agreed, and a meeting place was set. Not only did the two have time to meet while waiting for their flight, but they ended up signing a contract that helped us make our quarterly numbers for Wall Street.

Needless to say, the Synopsys salesman was amazed at the "miracle" I had pulled off—but not amazed enough to share his fat commission with me. Maybe next time!

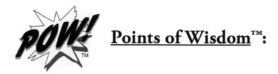 <u>**Points of Wisdom**</u>™:

- Take the time to build relationships with CEO assistants at other companies.
- Prove you're an effective partner by understanding the importance of requests that relate to the business.
- Gather all the facts and make a plan before setting up an important business meeting.
- If you have information or contacts, use them.
- Be ready to take on responsibility and accountability for the authority to make significant decisions.

THE FRENCH CONNECTION

Linda McFarland used her instincts when her CEO appeared doomed to miss a flight connection, which would mean that he would also miss a crucial meeting.

"The best way to predict the future is to create it."
– Peter Drucker

When I trust my gut, I always make better decisions, so I've made it a habit. As a result, some people have told me that I must be clairvoyant. I don't think I am. I simply pay attention to what's being said and, sometimes more importantly, what's *not* being said. I take body language into consideration, along with what I already know about the individuals involved. Then I try to keep an open mind and take appropriate action for a given situation. Call it "clairvoyance" or "trusting your gut"; it really doesn't matter. The bottom line is that it works.

I had the opportunity to practice trusting my instincts and making the right decision about three weeks after I was hired to support a CEO in Silicon Valley. At that time, he was traveling in Europe. Near the end of his trip, I received a call on my cell phone at about 11 p.m. I was surprised to hear my cell phone ring so late, but when I saw that it was my boss, I answered immediately.

My boss was sitting in an airplane on a runway in Madrid and had already been there for two hours. He was certain that he would miss his connection in France, and it was critical that he be back at headquarters the next day for an important meeting. He asked if I could check on alternate flights home, as it didn't look as though this flight was taking off anytime soon. Since they were so delayed, he suggested that I cancel his connection in France and find an alternative.

To this day, I can't explain why I said this to him next: "*I have a feeling* you'll make your connection. Just remember to run very fast when you land."

Before I could say any more, I heard him laugh nervously. I had been working with him for only three weeks, so he had no reason to trust *my* gut. His gut was telling him that he was going to miss his connection. He reminded me that the connection in France was due to depart in just 30 minutes. He was still in Madrid. The flight just to get to France would take longer than that. Simple logic dictated that we change his connecting flight.

But sometimes I get a feeling about these things, and I've learned to trust my gut. For some reason that I couldn't explain, I said, "I know I'm new, but I think you should trust me. You're going to make it. However, to make you feel more comfortable, I'll put a Plan B together, just in case things don't work out."

I could just picture him shaking his head and thinking, "What kind of 'Twilight Zone' assistant have I hired?"

He had his PDA with him, so I told him I would email him details of the back-up plan. He was very eager for those, as he was sure my Plan B would end up being his Plan A. He hung up, and I quickly called the after-hours travel agency.

It seemed as if I was on hold forever. Finally, an agent picked up. We discussed various alternatives and checked the departure status for the planned connection in France.

At first I thought my gut had failed me; the French connection was showing an on-time departure. "How very un-French-like," I said to myself. After all, this was the country credited with inventing the term "fashionably late."

We looked into alternative connections. They were nothing short of awful. If my boss had to take even the best of the alternatives, he would most likely be late for his meeting at headquarters the next day.

I asked the travel agent if we could book the best alternative as Plan B, but still keep the CEO's current connection, just in case a small miracle occurred. The agent must have believed in small miracles, too, as she agreed to hold both reservations.

I emailed my boss with the news, reminded him to run as fast as he could when he landed, and crossed my fingers that he would make his original connection. He confirmed receipt of the email and added that they were finally departing Madrid. Then I waited.

I tracked his flight on my computer. At 3 a.m., it showed that he had landed in France. I kept waiting to hear from him, but no word came through. I could stand the suspense no longer and finally emailed him, "Did you make the connection?"

I was so relieved when I got his reply: "I ran like crazy. I still can't believe I made it. This could only happen in France. Have to shut down now. Thanks."

What a relief…he had made it! Thank goodness the French were running fashionably late after all. I still don't know why my boss decided to trust me and run like crazy, but he probably figured he had nothing to lose. He told me later that if he hadn't run so fast, he definitely wouldn't have gotten on board. The flight attendant was just closing the door to the boarding ramp when he arrived.

From then on, whenever I said, *"I have a feeling…,"* he paid attention.

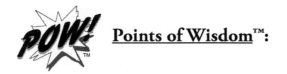 **<u>Points of Wisdom</u>™:**

- Use and trust your instincts (but have a back-up plan, too, just in case).
- On occasion, luck will be in your favor. You might as well take advantage of it.
- When you have a proven track record, your executive will trust your judgment.
- Communicate clearly and often.

THINKING INSIDE THE BOX

Linda McFarland used her diplomacy skills and the CEO's trust in her judgment to help modify what she considered some unprofessional behavior on his part.

"Change your thoughts and you change your world."
– Norman Vincent Peale

In order to make a point, some CEOs use language that I personally feel should not be used in a business environment. One CEO that I worked with was a frequent offender. Even though I had worked with him only a short time, we had already developed enough mutual respect and trust to give me the courage to suggest a change in his behavior. However, I knew I would have to make it a challenge for him, as he was nothing if not competitive.

After much deliberation, I went to a store and purchased a lovely wooden box. The box matched the décor of the CEO's office. I wrapped it and set it on his very tidy desk. I purposely didn't include a card to pique his interest. He arrived at work that day in the middle of a conversation on his cell phone and walked past me into his office. I smiled at him, but was a little disappointed, thinking that I would miss seeing his reaction when he opened the gift.

As he continued his conversation on the phone, I could hear him opening the package. I could also hear him telling the person on the other line about a mysterious box he had received. I decided to kill the suspense.

I poked my head into his office and whispered, "I'll explain the box when you are off the phone."

He smiled and said to the person on the phone, "Linda said she knows the story about the box."

He finished his phone conversation, and I stepped into his office and closed the door. I picked up the box and said, "I know I've been here only a few weeks, but you mentioned that I could come to you with any questions or feedback. Is that still true?"

"Of course," he replied.

The next question was a little tougher to ask, "Do you trust me?"

At that, he was a bit taken aback. But he said, "Of course," so I quickly continued.

"Every now and then, you say this one particular word that probably shouldn't be said around the office," I said, as diplomatically as I could.

I picked up the box and opened it. "I'd like to make a deal with you. Every time you say that word, I'd like you to put $10 in the box."

"Oh no," he said. "I think we're going to need to do some negotiating."

He immediately launched into his best negotiating tactics, for which he was famous. At least he didn't reject the whole idea outright, I told myself with relief. This was a new contest for him, and I was right that his competitive nature would take the bait.

Right now, the contest was about who would win the negotiation on the dollar amount of the penalty. Although adding $10 to the box would have meant a nice shopping spree for me, I allowed him to renegotiate to $1 every time he said the offending word. I consoled myself with the knowledge that he said the word so often that I should still be able to collect a tidy little sum. We agreed not to share this behavior modification idea with anyone else at the company.

"Now that you've decided what my job is, what's yours?" he asked. I told him that it was my job to spend all the money that he would be putting in the box. He laughed, and he went about his day determined to go home that night with all the money he had come in with.

Several hours later, he returned from a meeting in a sour mood. I greeted him with the question, "Do you need to put any money in the box for anything that you said during your meeting?"

"There will be no money for you," he replied.

Ah, I thought. This is a game for him. Although I'm sure he owed me a few dollars from the meeting, that wasn't the important point. The very existence of the box would serve as a behavior modification tool. I knew that every time he looked at that box, it would remind him of the behavior we had discussed. And over the course of the time we worked together, his language did improve—at least around me!

 ## Points of Wisdom™:

- As the executive's confidante, the assistant is a safe person to give the executive candid feedback that might be embarrassing to hear from anyone else.
- Don't hesitate to bring up an issue that is bothering you —especially if you think it affects the executive's image or future success.
- Be diplomatic when you provide feedback.
- Use your executive's nature (such as competitiveness) to get him or her to make behavioral changes, and be sure to make it interesting for your boss.

JUMPING THROUGH HOOPS

Bonnie Savage, CEO assistant, shares stories of how she satisfied some unique requests in a start-up company to make sure that the employees had fun, even in the midst of chaos.

"You don't always get what you ask for, but you never get what you don't ask for...unless it's contagious!" – Franklyn Broude

In the late 1990s, during the "dot-com" days, I worked for Mark Breier, the CEO of a start-up company.

Mark would frequently remind me that I was in charge of managing the company's fun. Fun was part of our company culture. Several times, I made trips to the nearby toy store to purchase foam dart guns that hung on cubicles all over the company. It was important that we always had that particular item available, as they were frequently used to build energy and camaraderie (never to settle scores or vent frustrations, of course!).

As part of the start-up environment, I was responsible for everything from having enough pencils around the office to organizing catering on a daily basis. The office was located in a residential area with few restaurants nearby, so that part of my job was especially challenging.

We held a company get-together every Friday. I negotiated with local vendors and even convinced some of them to deliver at no cost. As the deliveries would arrive, I was so excited about the potential of the company that I would give the company's elevator pitch to the poor, unsuspecting delivery person. After all, we were going to be huge someday; at least, that was my belief.

One particular Friday, the company meeting was scheduled at 2 p.m. Mark had been in his office working when suddenly he poked his head out and called to me around the corner.

"Bonnie, I was thinking that at the company meeting today, I'd like to present every employee with Lifesaver candy. Can you run out and pick up 350 Lifesavers?"

I thought to myself, "I can tell by the look in his eyes that he is absolutely serious."

I glanced at my watch and realized it was already 12:45 p.m. "I'll get right on it," I said. Then off I went to accomplish my assigned task. I knew the analogy of the Lifesavers was important because we had achieved a significant milestone for the company. Every time we did, off I would go to pick up some type of symbolic memento that tied back to the achievement.

This time, though, I needed help. There weren't many stores nearby, and picking up 350 Lifesavers would be no easy task. It was time to use my influencing skills. I hurriedly traveled through the building looking for any available administrative or facilities staff. Since we were in start-up mode, we were very aware that we would all be asked to do tasks outside of our normal job description without any notice. With no time to spare, I found a few willing volunteers. We divided and conquered, arriving back at the company meeting in the nick of time. I think we cleaned out the Lifesavers in every store within a 15-mile radius that day.

Of course, since I had pulled off the Lifesavers coup, from then on Mark assumed I could perform miracles on a regular basis. I don't recall the details surrounding all of these interesting requests, but I will always remember the enthusiastic staff that was there to help me track down 1,000 rubber ducks for our fountain to celebrate another exciting milestone. We called every toy, baby, bath, and department store in the area!

We not only built some lifelong friendships, but we also had plenty of fun during those exciting and volatile dot-com days. And needless to say, all my nieces and nephews have an endless supply of rubber ducks.

 **<u>Points of Wisdom</u>**™:

- Expect to wear many different hats in a start-up environment.
- Attitude is everything—especially where having fun and meeting momentous company goals are involved.
- When working in a start-up environment, remember to be flexible, resourceful, and enthusiastic. It's contagious!

JUST TRUST ME

There is almost nothing that comes up in a CEO assistant's world that requires confidentiality more than a merger or acquisition. In this story, Linda McFarland used the trust she had developed with her boss to make a highly confidential meeting about an acquisition take place at the only time when it possibly could – right now!

"Honor bespeaks worth. Confidence begets trust. Service brings satisfaction. Cooperation proves the quality of leadership."
– J.C. Penney

My company, Hyperion, had just finished a long strategy meeting during which a specific company was identified as a potential acquisition. This acquisition was a crucial piece to our overall strategic plan. Our CEO, Jeff Rodek, quickly followed up by placing a call to the CEO of the targeted company. They had a conversation and agreed that, due to the approaching end of the fiscal year, it was critical that they meet in person as soon as possible.

I joined in the conversation at that point to help determine when the two of them could meet during the next two weeks. To my dismay, the only time that worked on both of their calendars was—immediately. They were both available for the next two to three hours. After that, it would be weeks before their calendars would synch up again. There was no way around it; they had to meet now.

The CEO of the targeted company was finishing up some business near San Francisco. Jeff was at our corporate office about 40 miles south in Sunnyvale. They needed a location somewhere in the middle, a catered lunch, and complete privacy.

With my heart racing, I very calmly asked both of them to get in their cars and start driving toward Palo Alto, which was about halfway between the two locations. I promised to call them both back on their cell phones with further instructions just as soon as I had them. They both jumped in their cars and headed for Palo Alto from opposite directions. Talk about blind trust!

Once Jeff was out of the office, I remembered the Scotch that he kept in his office for guests. Somehow, that Scotch sounded really good to me right then. Then I remembered that I don't drink. Darn!

Instead, I told myself, out loud, "Go back to your desk. Settle down. Focus. And GET IT DONE!"

I got on the phone and called a contact, Audrey, whom I trusted. She managed catering at a hotel in Palo Alto. She picked up on the first ring. What luck! I explained my situation and the need for extreme confidentiality. She convinced me that she could handle it all with the utmost discretion and make it happen in less than 30 minutes.

I called Jeff and the other CEO back and gave them each directions. I also got their menu choices to make sure they would have as few interruptions as possible once their meeting started. Upon arrival, all they needed to provide were their names, and the attendant would direct them to the private room. They would be served their meals without even having to place an order.

Jeff and the other CEO held their meeting and accomplished what they needed to do. Not only was Jeff impressed with how I had pulled the details together so quickly, but the other CEO was nothing short of amazed. A few months later, the acquisition was announced.

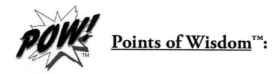

Points of Wisdom™:

- A foundation of trust is the key to a successful business partnership.
- If you have confidence in yourself and exude that confidence, your CEO and others will have confidence and trust you, too.
- There is always a solution to any problem, no matter how difficult the situation.
- Be bold. Make that phone call. You just might get what you want.
- If you believe you can accomplish the impossible, you can.
- Build relationships with your vendors, customers, and coworkers. They will be there for you when you need them.
- Keep your contact database up to date.

DON'T UNDERESTIMATE ME

A CEO assistant shares a story of how she used her influence discreetly and judiciously to deal with an executive's unethical behavior.

"I'm not concerned with your liking or disliking me...all I ask is that you respect me as a human being." – Jackie Robinson

Mary and I had worked together for many years at a previous company. We became friends and had tremendous respect for each other's work.

We found ourselves working together again later in our careers. Mary worked for one of the senior executives that reported to my CEO. From time to time, she would vent about his dismissive attitude towards her. She had heard him mention to someone at one point that she was "just an admin," so she shouldn't be taken seriously. That burned us both up.

But what really had her concerend was his ethics, and she shared those concerns with me. She couldn't pinpoint anything, but she knew that he wasn't totally playing by the rules. I knew this was something our CEO should be made aware of, but I needed concrete evidence before I could bring it to his attention.

The opportunity presented itself when the executive submitted an expense report and bragged to Mary about taking his whole family out for an expensive dinner while on a business trip overseas. He had written the dinner off as a customer sales dinner.

This was the evidence we had been waiting for. Mary gave the expense report to me. I took it to the CEO and pointed out the expense account abuse. He immediately asked to talk to Mary.

When Mary and the CEO met, Mary reviewed some of the other expense abuses she had witnessed. She explained that the executive had a car accident that he blamed on the company, because he was so tired from his hour-long commute each way. He decided the company owed it to him to have a limo pick him up from home every day for almost two months, and he wrote the expenses off on his expense account without ever having gotten anyone's okay.

With this information in hand, the CEO looked more deeply into the executive's expense reports and confirmed that the sales dinner didn't really happen. Shortly thereafter, the company's general counsel told Mary, "You might want to step away from your desk for a little while." After she had done so, they walked the executive out of the building.

Since no one ever told him what Mary had done, I'm sure to this day he has no clue how powerful administrators can be in that kind of scenario. He hadn't worried about bragging to her about his expense report, because he had felt confident that no one would listen to her if she decided to tell, because she was "just an admin."

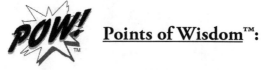 **Points of Wisdom™:**

- Pay attention to what's going on around you. If something doesn't seem right, investigate, and bring it to the attention of someone who can do something about it.
- Earn the trust of not just your executive, but your colleagues as well. They will be more willing to share confidences with you and request your guidance.

- If anyone says that you are "just an admin," realize that he or she has no idea of the complexity of the work that you do. Don't internalize their assessment of you. They are "just wrong."

REALITY CHECK

Hyperion's CEO was stranded in Europe during the 9/11 tragedy in the U.S. When he wanted his executive team to go through with a scheduled meeting as the horror of the World Trade Center unfolded on the television news, Linda McFarland had to take on the unpopular role of spelling out for him that the executives could not comply with his request.

"My whole career can be summed up with 'Ignorance is bliss.' When you do not know better, you do not really worry about failing." – Jeff Foxworthy

On September 11, 2001, I awoke very early to run a few errands before work. As I got into my car, I flipped on the radio. I heard the news about a plane crashing into one of the twin towers of the World Trade Center in New York. "How awful!" I thought.

When I arrived home from my errands and switched on the TV, my kids were awake and getting ready for school. I was just about to walk out the door when I saw another plane hit the second tower on the television screen. I said out loud, "Did that just happen? Is that for real? What's going on?"

My kids looked at me, hoping the events of the day would be a good excuse to stay home. I insisted that they get ready for school until we heard more news.

Once I got them moving along, my thoughts went ahead to the office. I was working at Hyperion at the time. I thought about all our executives that might be traveling, and in particular our CEO, Jeff

Rodek, who was in Amsterdam visiting customers. He was due to return home the next day. I was eager to get to work, but I also wanted to hear the news updates after I got there. I grabbed a portable radio and our small TV from home and headed out the door.

Our COO's assistant was already in the office making phone calls to the travel agency. We learned that we had several executives in flight. So far, we believed they were safe. All kinds of news reports were coming in. Planes were being rerouted. Despite all the activity, there was a sense of unreality that everyone who remembers that day shares. I felt as if we were all moving in slow motion.

Our executive team was scheduled at the corporate office for a two-day strategy meeting. It became harder to focus on the business at hand as the news reports continued to roll in. At one point, they called a break and gathered around a television. Some of the executives involved in the meeting lived in the New York area. They were concerned about family and friends. We were also concerned for the welfare of our customers, employees, and board members.

I telephoned Jeff in Amsterdam to give him an update. He had seen something about the towers briefly on his hotel room television, but he didn't know the extent of the situation. I asked him whether we should continue with the strategy meeting. I knew it was important, but I explained that everyone was distracted. Jeff felt it was best if we moved forward with the meeting.

I relayed the message to the team. I remember the surprised looks on their faces, as well as some of the comments they made. How could they focus when chaos was happening all around them? However, they agreed that the meeting was important for the company, so they resumed.

I went back to my desk with a heavy heart. Should I call Jeff back? How could I help him understand that an entire nation had changed in a matter of minutes? I flipped on the TV and learned that the situation had gotten worse. I decided that it was time to have a heart-to-heart talk with Jeff.

When I called Jeff, he was still at the Amsterdam office. I tried to explain the situation here. I added some comments about how the employees were feeling. I said, "Jeff, this isn't the same place you left just a few short days ago."

I went on to explain that people were worried about their families, their friends, and our nation's safety. "It's important that you find a TV so you can see what's going on here." With that, he agreed that he would return to his hotel room and take a closer look at the news. When we hung up, I was afraid that he thought I was overreacting. Of course, no one then knew what a tragedy 9/11 would become.

About an hour later, Jeff called. "I'm sitting here in my hotel room watching the news, and I can't tear myself away. This is unbelievable! Now I understand what you were trying to tell me. Please tell the executive staff to postpone the strategy meeting and take care of any personal issues they may have."

What a relief! Jeff understood now that it would be inappropriate to have a business meeting in the midst of national chaos.

Jeff then requested an update on the status of all our employees, customers, and board members vis-à-vis the World Trade Center. I had already gathered most of the information before Jeff made the request, so I was prepared. As I walked him through the update, he was relieved to learn that our employees and board members were all safe. Now I had the incredible task of getting Jeff a flight home, which is a story for another day.

Points of Wisdom™:

- Be sensitive and observant in extraordinary situations.
- Have the courage to speak up when you feel critical information may not have been communicated accurately or situations call for an alternative action plan.
- In extreme circumstances, gather detailed information so your executive can make sound decisions.

A DREAM OF A JOB

Some CEO assistants are accused of being clairvoyant. Debbie Gross knows her boss so well that she can often anticipate what he will say or do. But when she dreamt of an incident involving him that actually took place the following day, she began to wonder if she had gotten just a little too involved in her job for her own sanity.

"If you don't have a dream, how are you going to make a dream come true?" – Oscar Hammerstein

Sometimes as CEO assistants, our workload is all consuming. We are constantly thinking—and even dreaming—about situations at work. Not only do we dream of things that have actually happened, but we sometimes feel as though we are becoming clairvoyant, especially where our CEO is concerned.

Clairvoyance is not necessarily a bad thing. In fact, it can come in handy, although, as Debbie's nightmare illustrates, it can be painful to develop. But your intuition, if used with common sense and good judgment, can help you make excellent decisions and increase your ability to anticipate what's needed.

One night, Debbie had an unusual dream. In it, she was about to depart on a trip with her CEO, John Chambers of Cisco. He was in his office holding a briefcase. He told her that he really needed to bring it with him on the trip and asked Debbie to go outside and put it in the car.

When she got outside, there was a limo waiting. Debbie gave the driver the briefcase. She then went back to help the CEO finish getting ready, and they went outside together. She assured the CEO that she had put the briefcase in the car. As she turned to point to the car, she realized that the car was gone.

For the remainder of the dream, Debbie was frantically searching for the car and the briefcase, to no avail. Finally, she forced herself to wake up. Thank heavens it was just a bad dream!

That morning, Debbie arrived at the office at her usual time. Usually, John arrived later. This particular day, he had arrived very early. She found him already at his desk, writing intently. When she walked into his office, he seemed tense and barely looked up. When he did finally see her standing there, he said in his typical West Virginian drawl, "Morning, Debbie. You need to know that I'm working on a very confidential document that I need you to make sure is delivered to our partner today."

Apparently, John had been working on the document all weekend. He explained that he had not been able to sleep for several days, given the important nature of the project. He was told that the document had to be in his own handwriting. Once it was completed, she was to put the document in the briefcase that had been delivered for that purpose and ensure that it was locked. Someone would pick up the briefcase later that day.

Although Debbie could hear John talking, she realized that she was fixated on the briefcase sitting on his desk. It was exactly the same briefcase she had seen in her dream. With a voice that she couldn't quite keep from shaking, she told her CEO that it was one thing for him to challenge most of her waking hours, but it was quite another for him to invade her dreams as well!

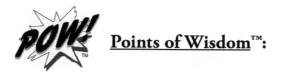

Points of Wisdom™:

- When you start dreaming about your work, it's time to get a life (or at least a vacation)!
- Don't be surprised if the synergy between you and your executive creates moments of clairvoyance.

IT WILL NEVER HAPPEN AGAIN

Joanne Linden shares an embarrassing, but enlightening, story about a trip when the Synopsys CEO arrived an entire day late in Taiwan, missing some crucial meetings as a result.

"Take chances, make mistakes. That's how you grow. Pain nourishes your courage. You have to fail in order to practice being brave." – Mary Tyler Moore

I was five months into my new job supporting Aart de Geus, Chairman and CEO at Synopsys. I was feeling comfortable in my new role, and things had been going smoothly...until today.

Aart was scheduled to attend a conference in Hawaii, and he decided that since he was already going halfway to Asia, he would extend the trip to visit customers in Taiwan. So I researched flights and was able to schedule one from Hawaii to Taipei on Saturday.

I informed the Taipei office of Aart's arrival time on Saturday evening. The Taipei office in turn scheduled meetings with government officials and tours of the city to occupy Aart all day Sunday. This was Aart's first trip to Taipei, and he was looking forward to seeing the sights.

Upon Aart's return from Taipei the next week, I inquired as to how his trip had gone. He replied that the meetings had gone well; however, there had been a slight problem. His flight into Taipei didn't actually arrive until Sunday night their time! The employees from the Taipei office and the government officials were there to greet Aart at his hotel on Sunday morning, but there was no Aart.

Aart, being ever so gracious, mentioned this to me only in passing, never making an issue of my mistake. I, on the other hand, was mortified. I had totally missed the small print in the travel agent's itinerary about the next-day arrival due to the time zone difference. Rather than going into the details of how it had happened to Aart, I simply apologized and said that it would never happen again. I immediately followed up with the Taipei office and apologized profusely for my error.

Aart never mentioned the error again; that is, until he attended my surprise birthday party five years later. So much for hoping he'd forgotten it! On this auspicious occasion, he chose to roast me in front of 50 guests by retelling the tale of how he had kept dozens of VIPs waiting in Taipei, thanks to my inability to read the fine print. He had so much fun sharing my very human failing with my friends and family (who all knew only too well how much I strive for perfection) that I barely felt the sting of realizing that an elephant—and a CEO—never forgets.

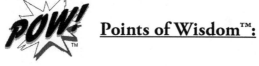 **Points of Wisdom™:**

- Read itineraries word for word after every change and take differing time zones into account.
- Take responsibility and apologize humbly to anyone affected by your mistake.
- Don't bore your executive with the details of how the mistake happened; fix it, learn from it, and move on.

UP THE CREEK WITHOUT
A PASSPORT

Linda McFarland relates the story of the time that her CEO lost his passport just hours before a vacation with his family. This story demonstrates the necessity of endless patience with one's CEO, as well as from one's own family.

"Patience, persistence, and perspiration make an unbeatable combination for success." – Napoleon Hill

It was a beautiful, sunny day in early January 2007. Only California has such sunshine in January. I was leaving work at a reasonable hour, for a change, to get home in time to take a walk with my husband. As soon as I got in the door, I kicked off my heels and changed into my walking shoes. Before my husband and I could get out the door, though, the phone rang. My son answered it.

"It's your boss," he called to me from the other room. I was surprised. My boss "Ted" was on vacation, and he rarely called me at home. After a brief hello, he asked, "Did I give you my passport when I returned from China?" I assured him that I didn't have his passport, but I asked him if he needed my help.

"I can't seem to find it at home, but I'll keep looking," he replied. "I'll call you if I need anything else. Don't worry about it."

Somehow I knew that wasn't going to be the end of it, and Ted would be needing me again soon. But my husband insisted that I leave my cell phone at home during our walk. Since there wasn't anything I could do at the moment, I complied. I will admit I was distracted during the walk, though, and more than once wondered aloud if I should go to the office and search for the passport. My husband chose to ignore those utterances.

When we returned home, I asked my son if Ted had called. What a relief; no call! With that piece of good news, my husband invited me to go out to dinner. I was a little apprehensive. I just had a feeling that I hadn't heard the last from Ted that night. But a date with my husband would be a welcome change. I decided to go.

I should have listened to my instincts. We had barely placed our order when my cell phone rang. It was my son. Ted had called and needed me to call him back as soon as possible. As I started to dial Ted's number, I could see my husband rolling his eyes. He knew our evening together was over.

"What's up?" I asked, when Ted answered the phone. He explained that he and his family had torn their house apart looking for his passport. It was nowhere to be found. They were scheduled to depart early the next morning for a ski trip to Canada. I knew that effective just that month, a passport was required to enter Canada or Mexico. What bad timing to lose a passport!

Before I could say a word, he said, "Here's the plan." I grabbed for a pen and paper, which in this case was the napkin in front of me. (Ted talks fast, so I knew I didn't have time to ask the waiter for anything else to write on.)

"My family is going to fly out tomorrow without me," he began in a rush. "I need you to figure out how to get me a new passport in the next 24 hours so that I can join them a day later."

"Let me do some research and call you back," I said. While we were talking, my food had arrived. When I hung up, I looked at my husband

and said, "I think this will have to be a quick meal." As expected, within two bites, Ted was calling again.

As I said hello, my husband wrote on a napkin, "The Devil Wears Prada," and held it up for me to read. I had to struggle to keep from laughing out loud. Ted *was* acting a lot like the Meryl Streep character in the movie that had come out the previous year—completely oblivious to anyone's needs but his own.

With some excitement Ted said, "I wanted to let you know that while I was talking to you, my family had a meeting. They decided that they don't want to leave without me. Once we have gotten me a passport," he continued, "can you work with our travel agent to change our flight reservations? Oh, and I'd like to change the reservations so that all of us can fly first class."

I was stunned. Did Ted have any idea what he was asking for? I pinched myself to make sure I wasn't dreaming, because I knew Ted was.

Ouch! No, I was awake. I was tempted to tell Ted that he was crazy and that my dinner was now cold. But instead, I said, "Let me see what I can do."

As I hung up, my husband asked, "Is there something I can do to help? If we need to drive to your office to look for the passport, I'll go with you." What a sweetie! Especially since I lived almost an hour from the office. But I shook my head. I had another plan in mind.

We asked to have the food wrapped up and headed home. I called one of the other assistants who lived near the office and asked if she would be willing to go in and look for the passport in several places that I thought it might be. I dropped my husband at home, kissed him goodbye, and told him I'd see him in a few hours. I headed for our other office closer to my home.

Once in the office, I checked the Internet for details about how to get a replacement passport. President Ford's funeral service had taken place earlier in the day, so I wasn't sure if federal offices were open. It wasn't looking good to get a passport replaced within 24 hours.

My cell phone rang. The other assistant was now at our corporate office. She wasn't having any luck finding his passport. I asked if his expired passport was in the file. Finally, a piece of luck: It was there. I asked her to put it in an envelope. I would pick it up in the morning or send our driver. I thought we might need it to expedite the passport replacement process.

I called our driver and asked him to pick up the expired passport early in the morning. I also asked him to be on standby in case I needed him to drive Ted to San Francisco to secure a new passport. We agreed to talk again in the morning. The most important thing was to pick up the expired passport. I called Ted to update him on the plan and then went home.

Early the next morning, I called the driver on my way to the office. He was already on his way to pick up the passport. I called my travel agent to check on alternate flights for the family. Hooray! There were morning flights that week with lots of availability. I called Ted's home and his wife answered. I let her know that I had our driver picking up Ted's expired passport to help with the replacement process.

Before I could even finish telling her the plan, she interrupted in a distressed voice, "Oh, my gosh! If I had known you had Ted's expired passport, we could have taken our flight this morning as scheduled."

So much for trying to be helpful! Instead of being a hero, I felt as though I had let down the whole family. Apparently, the conversation I had with Ted the night before didn't get passed along to his wife. That was unfortunate, because she had been the one dealing with their personal travel agent regarding the lost passport and possible cancellation of the trip. During their conversation, the travel agent told her that an expired passport could be used until January 23, 2007. If only I had had that piece of information before I went to bed last night. Their trip would be finished long before the January 23 deadline. Ted just needed his expired passport and driver's license for this trip.

Why hadn't I thought to check the details of the new passport regulations when I had talked to my travel agent? A lot of this nightmare could have been avoided. Unfortunately, that information never came up during any of my conversations with anyone. If only I had talked to Ted's wife the night before. If only, if only…

However, instead of letting my regrets overwhelm me, I immediately came back with a plan. "Are you packed?" I said. "There's a flight that departs at 11 a.m. out of San Francisco. I'll call the travel agent to check on availability. If we can get you on that flight, you can still leave today. If timing is right, about the time you arrive at the airport, I can have the driver meet you with Ted's passport. It's worth a try."

She agreed, so I hung up the phone and called the travel agent with the new information. Unbelievably, there were five first-class tickets available! We put the plan in motion. Next, I called the driver. With urgency in my voice, I said, "Instead of driving to Ted's home, head for the airport." I told him where to meet them and crossed my fingers.

As Ted's family arrived at the airport, there was the driver–expired passport in hand. Without a minute to spare, the family ran for the flight—and made it.

As I ate the remains of my cold dinner from the night before for breakfast, I began to fill out the paperwork for Ted's replacement passport. I was not about to get caught in this situation again!

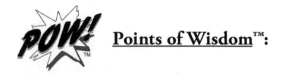

Points of Wisdom™:

- Be ready to make adjustments in a situation that is changing by the minute.
- Don't waste time "crying over spilled milk"; move on to the solution right away.
- Be careful not to get so absorbed in all the details that you miss a solution right in front of you.
- Stay current on travel regulation changes.

A DAY LATE AND MANY
DOLLARS SHORT

A CEO left his assistant a stack of work to take care of when he left on a trip. She had no idea that a time-critical request was buried near the bottom of the stack—a request that would ultimately cost the CEO thousands of dollars of his own personal money. Cindy Silva learned an important lesson that day about reviewing all tasks before digging in.

**"The greatest mistake you can make in life is to be continually fearing you will make one."
– Elbert Hubbard**

I had recently transferred to a new role supporting a high-profile CEO in a global computer-reseller company that was about to go public. "Fred" was intelligent, persuasive, and busy! This week was shaping up to be another hectic one for me. I had not yet perfected my interactions or effective communications with my boss. The handoff of his "to-do's" wasn't at all smooth yet, and his gruff delivery of commands didn't make it any easier.

One Tuesday morning, Fred was running late. A limo was waiting downstairs, leaving us no time to review important calls, appointments, or travel details before he departed on another trip. As usual, he threw a stack of work in my inbox on his way out the door, saying nothing about the contents. Before I could ask a question, he ran out to catch the car waiting to take him to the airport.

I continued with my busy day, making calls, sorting through my to-do list, scheduling and confirming appointments, replying to emails, etc.—all work that had been stacked up before he left. It wasn't until after 5 p.m. that I began to sort through the papers that Fred had thrown in my inbox. I found paperwork signed by my boss that needed to be faxed to a brokerage firm handling a "friends-of-the-company" pre-IPO stock offering for a company run by a CEO who was a friend of his. I faxed the order for 10,000 shares at the reduced price that same evening.

The next morning I arrived to find a voicemail from the broker, acknowledging receipt of the pledge to buy the stock, along with a very alarming message. He indicated that Fred had missed the deadline for the friends-of-the-company stock price, which had been 5 p.m. the day before. The stock was going public that day, and there was nothing anyone could do to get Fred in at the lower price.

I was horrified. My jaw dropped and panic set in. I called the agent and begged, but there was nothing that could be done; the deadline had passed and his hands were legally tied. I was extremely distraught that I had missed this important deadline. What was my boss going to say? Would I lose my job? Of course, the stock opened at a higher rate than what my boss could have bought in at, which was especially disturbing considering he was going to purchase 10,000 shares.

With tears running down my face, I ran to our VP of human resources to explain the situation. After he tried unsuccessfully several times to comfort me, I returned to my office. The president walked in and noticed my tears. He asked me what had happened. I told him my tale of woe, about the time-sensitive document and missing the deadline. The president felt so bad for me that he offered to give my boss 10,000 of the 20,000 shares that he had bought through the same special offering. What a sweetheart!

In the end, my boss didn't accept the president's generous offer for his 10,000 shares. I told him the truth about my blunder in missing the deadline. I offered a sincere apology and admitted that I had learned a huge lesson that day.

Thank heavens my apology was accepted. The silver lining was that he got a new understanding of the importance of improving the communication between us. I still can't believe he didn't blink an eye over losing so much money on that investment.

My boss and I went on to build a strong partnership based on communication and trust, which we both valued. We worked together for the next three years. I never made the mistake again of not at least skimming every piece of paper on my desk every day to see what fires I had to deal with, despite my heavy workload. That experience will remain forever etched in my memory.

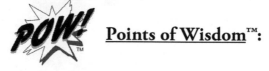 **Points of Wisdom**™:

- Have a system in place that helps you prioritize and reprioritize your work throughout the day.
- If you're new on the job, determine a process that works for both of you concerning communicating with your executive about important deadlines.
- When the worst happens, seek out the people you trust to confide in for comfort and advice.
- When you can't fix a mistake that you've made, 'fess up and determine to learn from it.

YOU DIDN'T KNOW THIS WAS THE INTERVIEW?

One CEO frequently relied on his assistant's informal conversations with candidates while they waited for their formal interviews with him. He had learned over time that she had a unique ability to "read" people, and he counted on her impressions to guide him in his decision-making. In this story, Linda McFarland describes how she developed and fine-tuned this highly valued skill.

"The beauty of empowering others is that your own power is not diminished in the process." – Barbara Colorose

While I was supporting the CEO of a local hospital, I realized the importance of the CEO assistant's role as a trusted advisor and confidante.

Several months after I was in this role, the hospital began to recruit doctors to the area. Part of the process included an interview with the CEO.

When candidates arrived to meet with the CEO, I would greet them and bring them to a small waiting area located inside my office. The CEO's office door opened into this waiting area. While the candidates waited, I would visit with them briefly. It's interesting what you can learn about a person in just a few short minutes. When the CEO opened his door, off they would go for their "real" interview.

At the end of each day, the CEO would come into my office, and we would review the calendar for the following day. Before departing, he would always ask what I had thought about the visiting candidates and what I had learned during my conversations with them. I remember him asking, "What does your gut say?" He seemed genuinely interested, so I told him.

After several months of candidate interviews, the decisions were made. He told me later that he had listened carefully to the feedback that I had shared. He had observed over the months that I seemed to have an ability to read people well. He would check his own radar against my feedback. I was both flattered and grateful that my opinions were valued so highly.

 **Points of Wisdom™:**

- You can establish the confidante element of your relationship with your executive when there is mutual trust, respect, and open communication between the two of you.
- Establish rapport with everyone coming into the executive's office. You never know when your opinion will be requested.
- Be observant even if you don't talk to your visitors. It's important to observe behavior and body language.
- You can gather great insight by seeking feedback from employees at all levels of the organization.

YOUR CARRIAGE AWAITS, MILORD

Debbie Gross, Cisco's chief executive assistant, had planned to send her CEO, John Chambers, to the White House in ground transportation that, unbeknownst to her, completely defied post-9/11 security protocol. In this story, she describes what transpired to help her save the situation from disaster.

"Acknowledge that you failed, draw your lessons from it, and use it to your advantage to make sure it never happens again."
– Michael Johnson

John Chambers and his wife took a trip to Washington, D.C., to attend a special dinner with key congressmen and political figures. This was their first time attending a White House dinner, and they were both quite excited. Shortly after their arrival at the hotel, John looked over the itinerary to make sure he understood the details for the evening.

John noticed that he was scheduled to take a cab for his ground transportation to the White House. He called me immediately. When I saw John's number pop up on my screen, I picked up and asked how his trip was going.

Skipping the pleasantries, he said in his West Virginian drawl, "Debbie, I was reading the itinerary, and I wanted to double check something. How will my wife and I be getting to the White House?" With confidence I said, "John, you're only ten minutes from the White House. My husband and I were just in Washington, D.C., and the hotel has taxicabs you can catch right outside the front lobby anytime."

John said, "Now Debbie (I always know there's something wrong when he starts a sentence with "Now, Debbie…"), how close do you think I will get to the White House in a taxicab, given the security that is in place for this dinner?"

Oh my! What was I thinking? I told John I would immediately arrange for a private car service and would call back with details.

Luckily within a short time, I was able to make all the arrangements. What a relief when he told me later that the event had been a great success!

 **Points of Wisdom™:**

- Always provide your executive with your contact information in case of an emergency or a change needed in the itinerary.
- If you're making arrangements for the White House or other high-security buildings or events, make sure you have the details regarding any special requirements, including identification or possible restrictions for getting in and out.
- Have your vendor information available and include it in the itinerary information.
- Review trip details with your executive, whenever possible, before he departs for his trip.

MISSION IMPOSSIBLE

At the last minute, Linda McFarland was asked to schedule a surprise trip as a gift from her CEO to his wife. The only problem was that it was far too late to get the accommodations he wanted.

"Formula for success: under-promise and over-deliver"
– Tom Peters

It was the Tuesday before Mother's Day, and our CEO made an unusual request. He and his wife loved to golf, and he wanted to surprise his wife by setting up a golf tee time the morning of Mother's Day—just five days away—on the world-famous Pebble Beach Golf Links. But the request didn't stop there. He had also extended the invitation to another couple that often played golf with them. Thus, the request (actually, more like a demand) was for two hotel rooms and a foursome tee time on the morning of Mother's Day.

That particular weekend is very popular at Pebble Beach. It's nearly impossible to get hotel reservations, and the golf course itself is usually booked weeks in advance.

After I got over my surprise at the short notice, I racked my brain for ideas. I remembered a contact I had at Pebble Beach. I had recently visited the area with some other executive assistants to tour a few of the hotels and facilities. I thought it was worth a try. I got on the phone, and my contact picked up. I explained the situation and held my breath.

To my disappointment, she explained that the Pebble Beach Golf Links were completely booked, but on occasion they got cancellations. She told me not to count on it, because there was already a waiting list. I asked if my CEO's name could be added to the list. I assured her that I would check with her daily about the status. I was determined to think positively and maintain confidence that everything would come together.

Next, I contacted the hotel. It must have been my lucky day. There had just been a cancellation, and I was able to secure two rooms that looked out onto the golf course near the ocean.

I provided my CEO with an update. He was concerned that they still didn't have a tee time, but I assured him that I would track the status of the golf situation daily. If the reservation for Pebble Beach didn't come through, I had made a back-up reservation at the Spanish Bay Golf Course nearby.

My CEO agreed with the plan, although he was still somewhat disappointed. I encouraged him not to give up. As of my last update from my contact at Pebble Beach, he was third on the waiting list.

The next morning, I made my daily call. There were some cancellations, and my CEO was now first on the waiting list. Unfortunately, he was still waiting. I reminded my contact that I'd check again the next morning.

The next day, before I could even place the call, my CEO was asking about the status. "I'll have an update to you shortly," I assured him. When I called, a cancellation had just come in. It was exactly what I needed – a foursome on the Pebble Beach course. Best of all, it was an 8:15 a.m. tee time.

With excitement in my voice, I called my CEO's cell phone and gave him the great news. "I had almost given up," he said with a voice of astonishment. "You're worth your salary many times over." I filed that compliment away with some others that he had given me. You just never know when it can get you a bonus.

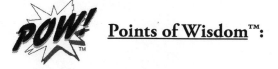 **Points of Wisdom™:**

- Expect tough challenges, especially near any holiday.
- When possible, visit hotels, resorts, and vendors in areas frequently used by your executive. You never know when you'll need a contact for a last-minute hotel room for a special occasion or offsite meeting.
- Think positively.
- Build your network with everyone you meet.
- Arrange a back-up plan.

WHAT IS IT WITH GUYS
AND CARS?

Good relationships with individuals outside the company can be a highly valuable resource. Bonnie Savage, CEO assistant, shares how she was able to deliver on a nearly impossible request because of the network she had developed.

"I feel that the greatest reward for doing is the opportunity to do more." – Jonas Salk

I was supporting a CEO who was traveling in Frankfurt, Germany, for customer meetings. After settling in at his hotel, my boss called to check in with me. We finished discussing pressing matters and then, with what sounded like hesitation in his voice, he mentioned that there was a huge car show in town. He had one free evening and was hoping that *maybe* I might be able to find him a pass for the event, even though he had heard it was sold out. What did I think?

I sighed to myself. What is it with guys and cars? I knew my boss was a huge car fan, but he was in Frankfurt, where the show took place, and I was in Silicon Valley. Who did he think I was—his fairy godmother? With a magic wand?

"I'll see what I can do," I promised, shaking my head as I hung up the phone.

After racking my brain, I remembered that I had one contact in Frankfurt. Although I didn't have much interaction with this contact, I recalled that he, too, was a car fanatic. It was a long shot, but I figured, what the heck? It wouldn't hurt to ask.

First, I did some research. I learned from another source that the event that particular night was for car dealers only. Getting tickets would be even more of a challenge than I had initially thought. My long shot was getting longer by the minute.

At 5 a.m. my time, I emailed my contact, explaining the situation.

My boss called later that day, hoping that I had made some progress. Unfortunately, I hadn't yet received a reply from my contact. I could sense the disappointment in his voice, but I reassured him that we still had time to pull this off. Since the request to attend the car show was unexpected, I still had my boss scheduled to return home on an earlier flight. If my contact came through with the tickets, I'd need to adjust his travel. Determined to be optimistic, I worked on a back-up travel plan while I waited.

An hour later, I received a reply to my email. I was very excited when I read that my contact had come through with the ticket. I immediately called my boss and gave him the good news. He was very pleased, especially when he learned that I had already put together a revised travel plan for his return home.

Everything turned out well. I later learned that my boss had even received VIP treatment for a sold-out, invitation-only event. I earned massive points that day.

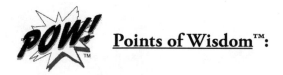

Points of Wisdom™:

- When you pull off a small miracle, the expectation may be for you to perform miracles often. Think of these as opportunities for growth.
- Even an infrequent contact can be a great networking resource.

CONNECTING THE DOTS

Linda McFarland tells a story about a CEO who was eager to set up a meeting with a high-level customer in Madrid. Unfortunately, she couldn't connect with the customer prior to the CEO's departure.

**"The way a team plays as a whole determines its success. You may
have the greatest bunch of individual stars in the world, but if
they don't play together, the club won't be worth a dime."
– Babe Ruth**

It was the beginning of another hectic week. "Any calls from that customer in Madrid?" our CEO asked, as he rushed by my desk. "Remember, this customer is critical."

As if I could forget! He had asked me that question every day for at least two weeks. I had been organizing an elaborate trip for him to Europe where he would be meeting with customers in several countries. ("If it's Tuesday, this must be Belgium," as the old movie title said.)

He was anxiously hoping to receive a call from our customer in Madrid before departing. Given the number of times he had asked me that question, it was obvious that this customer call was critical. The departure date finally arrived, but there had still been no call from the customer. He departed reluctantly, without that meeting on his itinerary.

Three days into the CEO's trip, my phone rang. I could see it was an international call on my digital display. I held my breath when I answered, hoping it was the much anticipated call. The accent on the other end of the line confirmed it. The executive's assistant identified herself and asked about the availability of our CEO for a face-to-face meeting in Madrid. To my disappointment, though, the time she requested was when my CEO would be in a different country. However, knowing the CEO's sense of urgency about this meeting, I began building rapport with the assistant while I bought myself some time to come up with a plan.

Glancing at the complicated travel schedule in front of me, I suggested some alternative times when my CEO would be in Madrid. The assistant on the other end didn't sound very optimistic, but I persevered. I asked her if she would please check the new options with her executive. In the meantime, I promised her that I would investigate what changes I could make on our end.

I hadn't made much progress in my investigation before I received a call back from the assistant with discouraging news. None of the days when my CEO would be in Madrid was going to work for them.

"Shall I cancel the meeting and try for another time?" the assistant asked. I debated with myself silently, then I made a decision. I told her that my CEO had stressed the necessity of a face-to-face meeting, and I asked her to hold the meeting date and time she had initially offered—at least until I could make some calls and get back to her. I knew this meeting was so important that our CEO would do whatever it took to make it happen. But I had a window of only a few hours to work out the details.

I hung up the phone and looked at the itinerary for the hundredth time. Our CEO was in flight at the moment, so there was no way I could talk to him or get his approval for what I was thinking of doing. My only option was to track down our salesperson in Madrid and bounce it off him.

I could hear the excitement in our salesperson's voice when I shared my news that the customer had finally called. We discussed a variety of options and schedule changes, all of which would mean an additional flight for the CEO—and an even tighter schedule than he already had. Finally, we settled on a plan. The salesman said he would work on rearranging the other customer meetings in Madrid to accommodate this new meeting.

"I'll call you back in the next hour," he assured me. "Wish me luck!"

As promised, he called back within the hour with the good news that the customers had agreed to change their meeting times. Now it was up to me to put all the puzzles pieces together to make everything fit.

I later learned that this meeting brought some important new business to our company. The CEO was delighted with the seamless way that the changes were made to his itinerary (if he only knew!) and the fact that they were accomplished in a very short amount of time. He was impressed with how I had "connected the dots" between the various meetings that had to be changed and the contacts that had to be made. He was especially pleased that I had taken these actions without even getting the opportunity to talk to him about it. His estimation of my skills and judgment rose substantially that day.

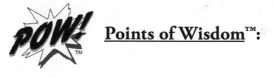 **Points of Wisdom™:**

- Making decisions with little or no direction can be intimidating, especially when they involve a customer meeting. Keep the company's best interests in mind and be confident that you are making the right decisions to keep your executive productive.
- Know the "who, what, where, when, and why" for critical meetings.
- Don't give up. Think on your feet and use every resource available.

- The choices we make are ultimately our own responsibility. Take ownership when you make decisions in the absence of your executive.
- Manage the small picture details, so your executive can stay focused on the big picture.

WHATEVER IT TAKES

When her CEO asked her to prepare a very special gift for each member of the board of directors for a meeting just 24 hours hence, Debbie Gross asked for the impossible—and got it! This story tells how.

"The price of success is hard work, dedication to the job at hand, and the determination that whether we win or lose, we have applied the best of ourselves to the task at hand."
– Vince Lombardi

John Chambers was traveling in Japan when he called me early one morning asking for some key corporate data. I always strive to have the data he needs available at my fingertips. With a twinge of excitement in my voice, I gave him the information. Immediately, we both realized that Cisco had just passed a key milestone. It was an incredible stretch goal that we had finally achieved.

Our board meeting was taking place the next day, and John wanted to do something special for the board to commemorate the achievement. "Debbie, could you pull together some type of unique gift for the board members?" he asked. "The gift should contain all the important milestone details. I'd like each board member to receive the gift."

I thought to myself, "Now John, you know I can't get a gift like that put together within 24 hours!"

Instead, I hung up the phone and immediately tapped into all my vendor contacts to see how they could help with this request. Most importantly, I needed a vendor that could deliver a unique gift within

24 hours. The plan was to have the gifts presented at tomorrow's board meeting.

After a few hours of telephone calls, I had a solution. One of my vendors (and now my new best friend) agreed to put together a beautiful prism. In addition to the milestone information, I wanted to give it a special touch. I asked the vendor to add each board member's name to the prism to personalize the gift.

Just prior to the board meeting, the gifts arrived. Whew—just in time! The packages were beautifully wrapped and ready for distribution. I had completely exceeded John's expectations for the gift. He was not only proud, but very impressed that I was able to find a way to deliver on such an extraordinary request.

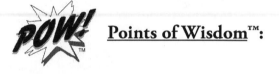 **Points of Wisdom™:**

- Ask for what you need, no matter how impossible. You just might get it.
- When you're asked to use your creativity, take a chance and use it.
- If you have an impossible deadline, work with people who thrive on challenges.

If you have similar stories you'd like to share for possible inclusion in our next book, please contact us at www.connect@planetadmin.net.

ABOUT THE AUTHORS

Linda McFarland has spent over 30 years mastering her "never-panic-under-fire" demeanor. She has held CEO assistant positions with a variety of Fortune-listed companies, spanning the high-technology, legal, and medical industries. With a passion for developing and training, Linda is a co-founder and member of the Silicon Valley Catalysts Association (SVCA), which is a group of CEO assistants. She serves on the advisory board of the Administrative and Executive Assistant Certificate Program for University of California Santa Cruz Extension in Silicon Valley and is a master instructor and guest lecturer for that program. Linda has delivered training programs to multi-national companies and has been an invited speaker at administrative and event planner conferences. She is a senior partner at PlanetAdmin, which provides consulting and training for administrative professionals. Linda currently holds the title of CEO Assistant at 2Wire. You can reach Linda at <u>Linda.Mcfarland@ PlanetAdmin.net</u>.

Joanne Linden has a background that spans more than 30 years as an executive assistant. With the majority of her career in Silicon Valley, she has worked for both successful start-ups and billion-dollar corporations. A true activist for professional administrators, she instructs at University of California Santa Cruz Extension in Silicon Valley's Administrative and Executive Assistant Certificate Program and is on the program's advisory board. Joanne is a current member of the Silicon Valley Catalysts Association (SVCA) and past president of the International Association of Administrative Professionals (IAAP), San

Jose and Crossroads Chapters. She is a senior partner at PlanetAdmin, which provides consulting and training for administrative professionals. Joanne currently holds the title of Chief Executive Assistant at Synopsys. You can reach Joanne at Joanne.Linden@PlanetAdmin.net.

ABOUT THE EDITOR

Sharon Turnoy has worked as an educator, editor, speechwriter, ghostwriter, communications manager, and CEO assistant in Silicon Valley. She is currently affiliated with Stanford University and welcomes comments at sturnoy@yahoo.com.

9294657R0

Made in the USA
Lexington, KY
14 April 2011